# The Cats of the High Peak Embassy Volume 2

## Sausage Rolls and Strategy

### Susie Halksworth

*To mum, who had a very challenging time over this period and dealt with it with her characteristic gallows humour and aplomb.*

# Contents

**Chapter 1**
A Useful Introduction: All You Ever Need To Know     5

**Chapter 2**
Winter 2023: Second Employee Lets Us Down Again     20

**Chapter 3**
Spring 2023: Tea and Tornadoes     44

**Chapter 4**
Summer 2023: Sausage Rolls and Spain     78

**Chapter 5**
Autumn 2023: Home Improvements     103

**Chapter 6**
Winter 2023-2024: the Goats are Not Helpful     129

**Chapter 7**
Spring 2024: Second Employee Is A Worry     151

**Chapter 8**
Summer 2024: Ghost is offered a Better Position     169

**Chapter 9**
Autumn 2024: A Beanbag Fulfils its Destiny     191

**Chapter 10**
Winter 2024-2025: The Employees are Snowed In     211

**Chapter 11**
Spring 2025: We have to be Terribly Supportive     224

# Preface

Thank you again to all the cats, Employees and other Random Humans on the Larry the Downing Street Cat for Prime Minister! Facebook group who have been so kind and supportive and nice about the first volume. I really hope you enjoy this one too.

# Chapter 1
# A Useful Introduction: All You Ever Need To Know

*Cough*. *Cough*.

Right everyone. Pay attention properly. Put down your cups of tea, your phones, and your copies of Take A Break magazine. This is Ghost, Feline Ambassador to the High Peak, with extremely useful information that you are going to want to make a note of. Now, I'm hoping that all you readers, especially Ape-Descended Employees who are not always very clever, have already read Volume One; so that you know what is happening and can pick up easily with this New Volume of our Clevernesses. But Esso said, you cannot assume things, Ghost; there may be all sorts of reasons why people are starting with the wrong book. For example they may have pressed the wrong button and bought it prematurely, and then not want to spend any more money until they know that this is a suitable book for them: and that they would not be better off spending their available funds on other books on Amazon. For example all those ones which involve Vampires acting inappropriately and against the laws of Biology.

Well, I approve of that, because it is thrifty (but I do not approve of books about Vampires. They are actually very boring people. I know a number of them: there is a small community living in Dove Holes, the village next door. I would not write books about them, personally. They are very preoccupied with the performance of their Pension Plans and with the effectiveness of various blackout blinds, in my experience). But, for you people who may have pressed the wrong button and who are now trying to make the best of what is potentially a difficult situation, you do not even know who Esso is. Imagine! You are *completely* in the dark. So, because I am a particularly Helpful and Kind Ambassador - everyone says so, even Second Employee's Mother - I have prepared a Handy Checklist of information which you can read and consider, and perhaps have to hand as you read the pages which follow.

I was going to set a test for when you had finished my Handy Checklist so you could self-assess to see if you were the right kind of person to benefit from this book, or if you needed to do a more extensive course of study first: but Esso said that was 'overly bureaucratic and off-putting', which shows you why I have the trouble I have, and why things here are not run as professionally as I would *ideally* like.

Anyway, I agreed not to do it, against my better judgement; but try to imagine that *my eyes are upon you sternly* as you absorb the wisdom in the following pages, because that might make you concentrate better and not, for example, wander off to make more cups of tea and eat Tunnocks Teacakes or watch Instagram Reels about people glossing their bannisters an unusual colour or some such nonsense.

**Ghost:** Ghost is me. I am Ghost. Ghost, me, is a cat. This is me, lurking behind Second Employee's Silly Elephant and looking out of Our Top Landing Window:

**Esso:** My brother Esso and I are cats who live in the Embassy. This is Esso, showing the lack of discrimination in soft furnishings which will, sadly, ensure he never reaches the Top Echelons:

Esso would like you to know *particularly* that he feels that one can see clearly from these very informative photos which I selected carefully, that we are actually the same colour; but that the black and white in our fur is distributed slightly differently. The kindest thing I can say about Esso's utter delusion in this respect is the following: *if* we are the same colour then it's quite a subtle effect, needing a high level of observational skills, which few people possess. In fact I think the only one who possesses them is Esso. So you may miss it. You may, instead, feel that Esso is black like the void and that I am an exceptionally pretty white cat with a black tail, three discrete patches of black on my furry back, and a small black smudge on my Tiny Precious Nosie.

I make no judgement on whichever conclusion you come to.

Anyway, Esso and I are Feline Ambassadors to the High Peak. We began our distinguished career at Chesterfield Cats' Protection, in Sue from Cats' Protection's Garage: and from there we were allocated our first Embassy, which is in Buxton, in a very special part up a hill near the drug dealer.

As you will, of course, already know, it is almost *unheard of* for Feline Ambassadors to be given such an important Embassy immediately: but, because we were so obviously incredibly competent, me especially, we leapt straight up the career ladder basically to the top. In fact, we leapt much in the same way I leap up onto the top kitchen cupboard and Second Employee says, Ghost, for the love of God come here, don't jump down via the open shelves and knock off all my Denby.

I am coming to Second Employee later.

As part of our Important Role, we share our Professional Briefings and Updates with Prime Minister Larry, and the Catinet, which is *quite clearly* the Governmental Cabinet of Cats, so please don't pretend to be unfamiliar with it. This has a number of benefits: it keeps everyone up to date with our Heroic Successes despite almost insuperable Challenges; it inspires others to do the same; and it educates those Ape-Descended Employees who may occasionally, and with very close supervision, be permitted to read by their Feline Employers.

This latter is obviously something we monitor closely, as it can be a double-edged sword: I have noticed that occasionally Silly Employees try to interact with each other by means of our Updates or, for example, through them become interested in the wrong things. This is of course difficult, and a drawback, and something which we have to weigh up: but Esso and I have decided that, on balance, our Updates are so Valuable and Intellectual that it is worth the additional trouble of, for example, Second Employee (who, again, *I am coming to later*) using them to talk to Other Employees in the comments and become inspired to crochet or preserve or paint something Exceptionally Silly.

So that is Esso and I. Two exceptionally fine, professional, and inspiring Ambassadors. Esso would like me to add here that rumours that he is 'always biting people and is really quite unpredictable' are just that, rumours, and have no basis in reality. I am a very truthful cat, and I would like to state, for the record, that I am here merely reproducing what Esso is saying without making any comment on it myself.

So that has entirely explained me and Esso. I would also like to explain to you the following:

**Buxton:** Buxton is a small, strategically vital, town in the mountains which is an almost unimaginable distance from Chesterfield, where we were born; and from which it is separated by TROLLS and GRUFFALOS and SPHINXES and GHOULIES and all sorts of BEASTS. The journey from Sue at Chesterfield Cats' Protection's Garage to Buxton was fraught with so many dangers and difficulties and heroic acts that no cats can ever recreate it and the journey has gone down in history, being the subject of a number of ballads of which three at least were composed by Esso. Second Employee says it is actually just down the A6 and then you go over the moors near Beeley and she does it all the time; but this is a flat-out LIE, and I include this statement only to show that Second Employee is an Unreliable Narrator and you must be sure not to trust a word she says.

Buxton is very cold and rainy but we have two weeks in July when it is sunny and then we all run about putting on Operas and Operettas and Fringes and Plays and Things, and Second

Employee sings Gilbert and Sullivan Patter songs when she is in the kitchen making cakes and also chases me and says, Ghost, come here and let me put sun cream on your Tiny Precious White Earsies.

**The Embassy:** the Embassy is a very tall, very narrow house. It has four floors, and Esso and I agreed when we moved in that I would have the top floor, the first floor, and a 50% share of the ground floor and basement. That has worked exceptionally well, apart from when Esso sometimes comes up to the top floor to PURR at Second Employee and CATALOGUE all the Silly Things on the big chest of drawers and LOUNGE on the Employee Bed, which was not the agreement; and that makes me cross.

First Employee says he cannot understand how he has ended up in a house which is composed entirely of stairs in a town which rains 90% of the time when he was previously living in a house in the Very Hottest Part of Spain in the manner of Marcus from Eldorado, which is a programme Esso enjoys watching on YouTube. I, however, can understand it. This is what happens when Employees make Bad Choices in their youth, and in fact this situation should stand as a lesson to other Employees to not spend all their money on Gin and Divorces, or, in the very specific case of Second Employee, Stylecraft Special DK Yarn.

**The Employees:** We have two main Employees, and also Interim Summer Employee who acts temporarily in role whenever the other Employees go away to First Employee's House In Spain. I understand they do this so that Second Employee can have a meltdown in a different country and insist on buying flights back early via Ryanair even though there is no 4G on the mountain and you can only really get wifi if you go to Peppa's Bar and lean out of the window with your phone while you are having your Churros and Café Con Leche. Interim Summer Employee is the best and most efficient Employee and always very responsive when I shout at him: but Esso says, Ghost we cannot be disloyal and we have to keep the two original Employees as well, we cannot just get rid of them. Well, I personally am waiting for a new Government to get rid of all employment protections and we will see how loyal I am then. But I digress.

I have occasionally been asked why we called the Employees First Employee and Second Employee and if it is because First Employee is older, taller, more efficient generally, or more likely to wear something which has been ironed. Although all these things are true, they are not the reason. We actually called the Employees First and Second Employee after the order in which they were introduced to us at Chesterfield Cats' Protection. First Employee came into our garage first to say hello to us and make clicking noises with his tongue, while Second Employee was still FAFFING about outside. We could hear her talking to

Sue about Lucky, a co-resident, who had been returned three times after his three new Employees had all died, one after the other. Second Employee was saying how unfortunate this was, and what a massive shame for poor poor Lucky.

So this straight away shows you the level of naivety we are dealing with.

Anyway, fortunately for Second Employee, Esso and I took them both on before Lucky could claim his fourth and fifth victim. And really, it has been a mistake. I mean I have to look at this objectively and say to you that Second Employee has no more ability to deliver on her KPIs than she has to abseil down the side of Buxton Crescent. Esso says I have to make it clear that he and Second Employee are Special Best Friends and he loves her very much and he PURRS and he is her Precious Velvety Boy and Special Chunky Chonker: but, as I say to him, nobody cares about this. As an Employee she has not delivered.

I will say to you in confidence that Esso was taken away from his mother a little too early, and he has a tendency to become deeply attached to anyone who shows him gentleness or affection: obviously this is terribly poignant, but, more importantly, it is completely disastrous in terms of staff management. It means Second Employee has been allowed to get away with a lot of NONSENSE. For example, she has painted the Embassy ridiculous colours. She crochets ridiculous things. She bakes ridiculous items. She adds nothing to Strategic Plan delivery. I have still not given up hope of getting rid of her.

First Employee is more efficient. He has To Do Lists. He walks purposefully. He wears a suit, and owns a phone which he can tap-tap-tap do useful things on because all its memory has not been used up with hundreds of photos of Esso with his leggies in the air at very slightly different angles. He says, Susie, have you emailed the management company/ sorted out the insurance/ contacted the solicitor, and then Second Employee looks shifty and says, shall I make us a nice coffee, I have baked stem ginger shortbread. I cannot understand why - or how!  they are married. My only explanation is that they must have both been sitting randomly on a bench together, suddenly both decided spontaneously yet independently that they would like the tax benefits specific to matrimony, turned to look at each other, and taken the line of least resistance. I am almost sure that is how it came about. I cannot understand how else it could have happened. It is clearly a process which should be Rationalised by Cats!

Anyway, that is the Employees for you. I suffer greatly.

**Second Employee's Parents:** one of the problems with both the Employees which we didn't originally anticipate is that they both know lots of people who all come and TROOP into the Embassy and look at Esso and I and say, look at your cats over there, as if we did not realise what or where we were. And actually, they are wrong: we are at least 75% House Demon from Granny on our Mother's Side, but Esso says I have to not say this now we have professional careers so you had perhaps better forget I mentioned it.

Anyway the most frequent of these Silly Visitors are Second Employee's Parents who are always LURKING somewhere around the Embassy, sitting and drinking tea and eating biscuits and looking what is going on.

Second Employee's Father is a person who is ALMOST UNIQUE in that family as being someone who can Cope With Cats: and Esso would like to reiterate that he did not bite him, and was not responsible for his subsequent hospitalisation, and that this is a *key fact to know* in relation to this subject. Again, I reproduce Esso's statement without comment or corroboration. Second Employee's Mother has still not forgiven Esso for the occasion alluded to in the previous sentence but one.

**Second Employee's Brother:** I do not approve of Second Employee's Brother. What is he doing being an Artist? What kind of nonsense job is that? Is he appropriately qualified? And what kind of artist paints Hyperrealist Sausage Rolls?! Honestly, it makes me cross just thinking about it.

**The Goats:** really this is slightly embarrassing but I suppose I should mention it. The Goats were living in Andalucia, but they fancied a change: I pulled strings and helped them with flights and visas on the Strict Proviso that they also helped me Quid Pro Quo with certain personal difficulties. Well, look, specifically I wanted them to help me with declaring WAR on Second Employee's Brother because I really find him very annoying and I do not approve of his silly sausage rolls, I have already specified what is a suitable subject for ART and processed meat products *are not it*. As I have *said*, I will allow art of noble and predominantly monochrome cats striking interesting poses, fields with or without sheep, and vases of flowers. You may wish to make a note of this as it is surprising how often it becomes an issue.

Anyway whatever the correct definition of art is (it is mine), the GOAT situation has, unfortunately, not worked out properly. The goats have been a disappointment. I do not talk of them. Actually, that's reminded me that Alejandro, the Goat Leader, has invited Esso and I to a fondue party next Friday at the Goats' cottage on the Thornbridge Estate down the road. I might go, because I do like fondue, but I shall *disapprove* the whole way through.

Right. That has been a whistle stop tour around the world of the Embassy and our Important Work. I hope that has completely clarified everything for you, you have absolutely no questions or confusion remaining, and that you will now understand entirely what is going on when you read the following Important Pages, and are ready and able to benefit properly from our WISDOM. Make sure you read carefully and take notes as appropriate - this is a level of information that Ape-Descended Employees don't often have access to! You are extremely lucky!

[Everyone - this is Esso - look, I'm really, really sorry. Ghost said to me, *Esso, I am going to do an Informative Introduction for anyone who has wandered over here Willy-Nilly without reading Book One first, because some people are like that, like Second Employee who has to read the ending of books first to check they end happily before she gets emotionally invested, because she is mad*. Well I thought it sounded like a good idea, but I should have known she'd just use it as an excuse to air her prejudices. Could you just ignore anything she's said that seems a bit negative? Many thanks. I've talked to her about it. Here's my alternative Introduction:

We - Ghost, my sister, and I, Esso - are the Feline Ambassadors to the High Peak. We update Prime Minister Larry on our progress with bringing Order and Gracious Living to Buxton, through Public Updates which we have now been persuaded to publish because they are so Improving and Informative. We have two Employees, First and Second Employee, and also Interim Summer Employee. We love them all so much! I love Second Employee more than anything in the world, and I follow her round and PURR and she strokes me and says look at you Mr Esso, you're my fabulous Chunky Chonker. We're all very happy here in Buxton. It does rain a little bit. I don't love Second Employee's Mother quite as much as I love everybody else. I hope you enjoy our Updates!]

# Chapter 2
# Winter 2023: Second Employee Lets Us Down Again

**January 2023**

Larry and the Catinet: this is Ghost, Ambassador to the High Peak, with an Exceptionally Important Update. Larry, Second Employee has gone quite mad, and I need her to be dealt with quickly, because, as I'm sure you can imagine, having a Mad Employee wandering about reflects on us as Feline Employers extremely badly; on me in particular. To be frank, I think Esso looks like exactly the type who would have a Mad Employee, but I definitely do not. So this whole situation will need to be sorted out very quickly.

It began when Second Employee found a dress she liked in the Boden Sale, which she said would make her look like Wednesday Addams. Well, Larry, there is no chance of Second Employee looking like Wednesday Addams unless she magically becomes thirty years younger and a good four stone lighter, and I believe that to be out of the scope of a dress:

although Esso says I am being uncharitable, and even though Wednesday might be going it a bit she could well have looked like Morticia after a slightly hard morning and a good few months on the CAKE. Esso is too fond of Second Employee, so does not have the right attitude to things. I tell him this often. It's best not to get attached to the staff. Anyway, Second Employee decided not to buy the dress, which was a good job as it was UTTERLY IMPRACTICAL; almost as bad as the one she bought recently in pastel colours, with Elvis Presley on the fabric and a FRILLY COLLAR, which I notice she has not worn yet. However, she did not decide not to buy it for a sensible reason, but only because 'she would be damned if she was going to pay that much for 100% polyester'.

Well, Larry, this set her off on a Very Silly Train Of Thought, which ended in her deciding that clothes were more expensive and worse quality than they ought to be, and probably produced in Unethical Circumstances, and because of this she was going to - wait for this, Larry, I bet you can see where we're going with this - make her own.

Larry. I can't have this. She has knitted a Fuchsia Cardigan, which just looks ridiculous. Esso says it is not ridiculous, and he likes to KNEAD on it because it is very soft: and its success is due to all his hard work in Airing The Wool, by wrapping it round all the chair legs in the dining room and kicking it under the sofa.

Larry, what does Esso know about Aesthetics! Neither he nor Second Employee can be trusted. Second Employee owns a large clutch bag, in rainbow fur, which has eyes. I have seen it. I was not impressed. And to make things worse, Larry, Second Employee has taken to going for walks, even when I am waiting to do her Daily Appraisal, because 'no-one in this house understands that she is an introvert and needs quiet time'. So while she is walking about being RIDICULOUS and SELF-INDULGENT, of course she meets and strokes all the neighbourhood cats, and they report back to me. Only last week, Mrs Tiggywinkle from Lightwood Road said to me, I saw your Susie the other day, Ghost, she looked well enough although I'm not sure about those dungarees.

Well I cannot have Mrs Tiggywinkle, in particular, calling Second Employee by her informal, silly name and making comments on her clothing choices, however correct she might be (she is): so I have decided that I shall institute a uniform for the Employees. Esso says he would like them to wear 'something lovely and soft that he can knead on, like Second Employee's nice jumpers', which is silly: I am currently thinking along the lines of grey suiting in a fine wool, and possibly also a summer uniform in deconstructed charcoal linen to be worn for the two weeks in July when it (sometimes) stops raining. I imagine, Larry, this might be an idea that others in the Catinet might wish to adopt: I shall begin by reaching out to a few select Scandinavian Minimalist Designers, and I'll be in touch again when we're at the fabric sample stage!

**January 2023**

Larry and the Catinet: this is Esso, Ambassador to the High Peak, with my Instructive Update. Larry, Ghost gave me news earlier that Activated My Ears; apparently, despite all our predictions, Second Employee had gone to Parkrun without being properly briefed by us, and may well have made a Terrible Show of herself.

Larry, Second Employee failed to heed the very wise words of her cousin's ex-wife, who once said: do not ever go to an organised run in the rain, because it will be full of Keen People and no-one else, and you may well come last; whereas if you go on a nice day there will likely be someone there in a Chicken Costume who you have a fair chance of beating. Fortunately, when Second Employee returned looking like a Drowned Rat in her Aldi Hoodie, she explained to us that she had been forced to go, because First Employee had woken up with her and had decided to get up too, and she hadn't had the heart to look him in the eye and tell him she had changed her mind when he had got up at 7:30am on a Saturday specially to support her. So we have withdrawn our objection about the lack of planning and briefing by us, and Ghost is writing an extra appendix for the Strategic Plan to deal with all future Parkrun issues in case

Second Employee ever decides to take leave of her senses and do it again. We think it is vanishingly unlikely: but, you never know.

Larry, also, First Employee has caused us all sorts of problems recently, when he is normally so reliable! A few weeks ago, he did the most shocking thing you can imagine. He looked at something called a Smart Meter, which is a small black thing with numbers which is normally hidden on the bookcase behind a particularly improving book by George Monbiot which Second Employee really ought to have read and hasn't, and said this *could not continue*; and we had got to Take Action on Reducing Drafts. So we all had a conversation about heavy curtains, and then he insisted on closing the Sitting Room Door, and said Ghost and I would have to ask to be let in or out.

Well, Larry, as you know, Ghost Cannot Be Trammelled: and Second Employee could not cope emotionally with Trammelling Ghost: so Second Employee refused to sit in the Sitting Room any more, and she and I and Ghost all sat downstairs together with the electric heater on, with First Employee on his own in the Sitting Room, without any drafts, but also without any family. So First Employee said this could not continue either, but, instead of him giving up and having the door ajar as it was before the silly Smart Meter, we woke up one day and the door was shut, a new cat flap was in it, and First Employee was sitting on the other side of it, thinking he was very clever!

Well, you can imagine what Ghost thought. She spent the first three days Guilting Second Employee, by touching the catflap sadly and impotently with her paw and then Squeaking, even though she uses the ones in the porch and the outside door quite happily: but, unfortunately, she was sleeping under the sofa one day when Second Employee wandered off upstairs, and Ghost SHOT out of the catflap after her to see what was going on, and Second Employee saw her do it: and now Second Employee knows that she can use it perfectly well, she just *does not want to*. So now Second Employee says to her, Ghost, am I your trained monkey, and Ghost is annoyed because she says if Second Employee actually was a monkey she might be a bit more efficient, and can I not get her a monkey on either eBay or perhaps from the drug dealer down the road. Well, Larry, I haven't managed it yet, but I do hope you'll agree with me that it probably wouldn't be a good idea *anyway* to introduce a Monkey into the Embassy, especially if it is going to be more efficient than the Employees. I do think we need to think of morale.

But, most annoyingly, First Employee has had to start working in Second Employee's Room because the Employees are FAFFING ABOUT with the laminate flooring in his: and when Ghost went to talk to him very seriously about arranging his Second Floor induction, he told Second Employee that Ghost had 'come to see me and miaowed and miaowed, which was very sweet'. Ghost is FURIOUS at being patronised and not listened to, especially since she is in charge of the Second Floor and *technically* responsible for all his actions; and without his induction being signed off formally we are very unsure as to whether he will be covered by our Public Liability Insurance. Larry, it is all terribly difficult! I have decided that the *very best action I can realistically take* is to have a long nap on the sofa downstairs, against the radiator, and to get some purring done: and then I'll be in the best shape possible to tackle anything that comes!

**January 2023**

Larry, and the Catinet. This is Esso, Ambassador to the High Peak, with a brief update. Larry, Second Employee and I have been Looking Through Old Photographs, and have found one of Ghost and I right at the beginning of our careers when we had just arrived at the Embassy. I would like to discuss this, because I think it is instructive for the Catinet and their Employees to understand how Ambassadors, who might begin by being quite small and with perhaps rather disproportionate ears, can become Respected Establishment Figures like Ghost and I, *solely* by means of dedication to the delivery of the Strategic Plan.

Some of us (me) think it is difficult to tell us apart in the photo. Others of us (Ghost) are very rude about the situation, saying, Esso, you are almost entirely black like a VOID or a SHADOW and I am entirely white with the most beautiful three black spots, a black tail, and a black smudge on my NOSIE in a way which has been much admired. I find this a reductive way of looking at things, however: instead, I think it needs a subtle, artist's eye. Although, Ghost would want me to add here, not an artist like Second Employee's Brother, who she disapproves of most profoundly. An artist who paints things Ghost has sanctioned; for example, and I am quoting her here, 'proper fields with sheep in them or a vase of flowers, Esso, not bloody hyper-realistic sausage rolls. Sausage rolls! I don't know what he thinks he's doing with that kind of nonsense'.

I am on the right as you look at the photograph, and I have a calm yet resolute expression: and Ghost has stretched her front LEGGIE over my tail, possibly in order to reach out to whoever was taking the photograph, in order to solicit biscuits, stroking, or our favourite childhood toy, the Giant Peacock Feather. If you look very, very closely, it is perhaps possible to see that the distribution of black and white in our fur is very, very slightly different, I suppose: but, personally, I can barely tell. It really is extremely subtle.

I do hope the Catinet and their Employees find this Trip Down Memory Lane instructive, Larry, and that it may encourage some of the more recalcitrant Employees to strive to be better! It has unfortunately not encouraged Second Employee: she merely said to me, look at how tiny you were, Esso, and now you're a massive Mr Chunky Chonks; and then she kissed my Nosie: but I am used to Subtlety and Improving Situations going straight over Second Employee's head, and luckily she has other redeeming qualities!

## January 2023

Larry and the Catinet, this is Ghost, Ambassador to the High Peak, with my update which is always more useful than Esso's. Honestly, Larry, I don't know what nonsense he has been telling you: but luckily I'm here now with my Razor-Sharp Mind and Unparalleled Observational Powers.

Well, I have had Two Excellent Ideas this week, Larry, both involving ways of saving *enormous* amounts of money which will stop the Employees BLEATING about the Cost Of Living Crisis and the Pies in Waitrose being 50p more expensive every time they buy one. I mean, obviously in any sensible world they would just stop buying the pies from Waitrose, but I am not going to suggest that at this juncture because I, personally, have known Second Employee in particular to throw Caution and Thrift to the wind and go buying pies in the Chatsworth Estate Farm Shop: and, if she does that, she often comes back with Cheesecake and All Sorts, too, and then we may as well, frankly, all go to hell in a handcart.

So, I have got an alternative idea. I shall use the following example as illustration. This week, Second Employee found from somewhere or other and brought home in triumph a Very Silly Lamp Base, which she has stated that she believes to be 'Bitossi-inspired'. Larry, that Lamp Base is inspired by Bitossi in the same way that Esso is inspired by Panthers or Second Employee is inspired by people who can run 5k in under twenty minutes: i.e. pointlessly, because there is *no discernible effect of the inspiration*. First Employee says it is possibly the ugliest lamp base in existence, which is true, and I am sure Second Employee will at some point manage to source a lampshade which will make it look even worse. But, Larry, here is my point: he says this in an amused, indulgent kind of way which I *personally* feel downplays the seriousness of the matter; and while I was disapproving of his tone, the following thought came to me: why do we allow Second Employee to have access to her own money at all?

After all, she's always wandering home with nonsense: for example, that ridiculous large crocheted spider which Esso nuzzles against to go to sleep even though I have told him not to: all sorts of silly plants, wool, and dresses with pictures of Elvis on them. We do not need any of these things. I have decided the best thing to do is to take away Second Employee's credit card, so as soon as I get a moment I will send you the number, Larry, and I would like you to cancel it and perhaps put a trace on it so that if she attempts to use it she will be immediately taken Right To Prison. I think this will probably go at least 40% of the way towards offsetting all this Cost Of Living Nonsense!

But, luckily, because I am an Exceptionally Clever Cat, I have also got another idea which will deal with the other 60% and possibly even beyond! The idea came to me the other morning. The Employees were sitting together in the kitchen drinking coffee and eating Poached Eggs: Esso was asleep with Boris the spider on his sofa: and I was PATROLLING around near the freezer to see if anyone unauthorised had been in the kitchen overnight and if I needed to pee underneath it to put them off.

As an aside, Larry, I do think I do all of the heavy lifting with Territorial Peeing, and it is quite a faff sometimes to ensure I am always sufficiently hydrated. I really feel Esso or even First Employee could take on some of the burden occasionally (Second Employee would never get the aim right, especially in some of the more challenging positions). Anyway, I was concluding that it was all ok for the moment and so was manoeuvring my bum away from the freezer, when I heard the Employees talking.

First Employee had opened a letter about the renewal of the health insurance for Esso and I, and was telling Second Employee how much it cost: and then I heard him say, very distinctly, 'so, Esso is much more expensive than Ghost!'

Second Employee was surprised, and said, why is that, and First Employee said, I don't know, I imagine it is based on an assessment of relative risk, and I imagine generally male cats are more adventurous.

We all looked at Esso, fast asleep on his sofa, pressed against the radiator, with all his LEGGIES in the air. First Employee said, that is because they have not met Esso, and Second Employee said, yes, it does seem a little unfair. However, Larry, I have been thinking: unfair or not, and I am absolutely not going to get Esso started AGAIN on sex-based discrimination, if it costs significantly more money for Esso to live here too, I think there are perhaps hard decisions that could be made. And I think possibly the result of those hard decisions, which may or may not involve Esso going to live, perhaps, in a housing estate just outside Stockport, might also have the added bonus of freeing Second Employee up hugely so she can devote more time to stroking me. Because she would not forever be distracted by Esso following her and PURRING and NUZZLING and wanting to sit on her lap in a way that some cynical people might construe as needy. So I think you can see that some hard decisions might not only solve the Cost Of Living Crisis for the Employees *at a stroke* but might also FINALLY make Second Employee an effective Employee!

I shall leave you to think about that, Larry, and in the meantime I shall not say anything to Esso, because there is no need for him to start querying things and being difficult before it's all sorted out and there's no going back!

**February 2023**

Larry and the Catinet. This is Ghost, Ambassador to the High Peak, with a MAJOR COMPLAINT. Larry, Esso has hurt my feelings terribly. He and I went to the VET to have our BOOSTER for whatever completely unlikely disease Second Employee has decided we are going to catch in our back garden - I *personally* think the only thing we're likely to catch is Incompetent Pruning and Mismatched Container Disease, but there we are - but as Esso says, it keeps Second Employee happy and stops her worrying about us and FAFFING. So we go with a good grace.

Now the funny thing is, Larry, that even though we have been to visit the Vet before and I know there is nothing to worry about, every time First Employee puts me in the large cat carrier (because I cannot be trammelled) and squashes Esso into the small one, my mouth always begins to sing the I Do Not Want To Go To The Vet song, even though my brain says there is no need. I do not know why it is, but Esso says, never mind, Ghost, just go with it and we will adjust the Strategic Plan Appendix J subsection 24 (Vet Visit Etiquette) accordingly. Anyway, here is where Esso hurt my feelings. He said, can I just mention to you, though, Ghost, you're actually supposed to sing Miaaaaoooowwww, not Meeeee-ooooooo. Meeeeeeee-ooooooo is the incorrect pronunciation. I hope you don't mind me mentioning it, I just don't want you to sound a bit gauche in front of the Vet.

Well, Larry, my feelings are hurt dreadfully, can you imagine. Calling me gauche! When I *personally* have had to explain to Esso in the past how to pronounce Cholmondeley and Belvoir, when he was in danger of making himself look quite foolish at the AGM of the North Buxton Monochrome Cat Alliance! And then, Larry, it got worse. When we were in the consulting room, discussing our health with the Vet, and I had been taken out of the carrier and examined, which I *do not like*, I decided I would have a break for a moment and go and stand behind a sheet of plastic which was propped against the wall. I will confess, I was hoping to become invisible for a moment and redirect the attention, which at that point was focused on my GUMS, perhaps to Second Employee: but unfortunately my mouth began to Meeoo! Meeoo! again, and everyone laughed and said, Ghost, there is no point trying to hide behind there and miaowing as well, we can all see you, you've forgotten to tuck your tail in! Then the Vet very rudely lifted the sheet of plastic away, so I was REVEALED, and everyone laughed again!

Larry, perhaps it is true that I had, for one single time in my hitherto unblemished career, made a bad choice: but I think if we are talking about bad choices we could perhaps look elsewhere. We could look, for example, at the time Esso ran across the porch floor when Second Employee had just painted it blue and had Silly Blue Feeties for a week, or when he walked across the hob and turned on the gas when Second Employee's Brother was looking after us, which led Second Employee's Brother to worry that 'Esso would blow the whole street up on his watch'. Or we could look at when Second Employee ran away from her house in Cambridge with nothing sensible at all, mainly a pack of Tarot cards with cats on them, and not even enough knickers, so she ended up in a Travelodge wearing leopardskin pole dancing shorts: and then married First Employee almost entirely randomly and without remembering to ask him first whether he talks a lot. Or when the Employees last week bought a carpet without measuring the room properly, and with quite predictable results.

So if we are thinking about bad choices, Larry, I hear things, and I know things, and I remember things, and everyone would do well to think about that when they are laughing at me Mee-oooing and not tucking my tail in. Because the visit to the VET is stressful enough, Larry, without mockery, however affectionate Esso says it is. So if you would treat my COMPLAINT as a FORMAL GRIEVANCE, and act accordingly, I would be very grateful!

## February 2023

Larry, and the Catinet, this is Ghost, Ambassador to the High Peak, with a brief update, because I am currently a Very Busy Ambassador. Larry, I do not ever want to make passive-aggressive comparisons between, for example, my level of commitment to the effective delivery of the Strategic Plan and Esso's level of commitment to lying about, sleeping, purring, and headbutting Second Employee: but, if I *were* to do so, I think we might all find it rather telling. Earlier, Larry, I asked myself, where is Esso? As I did a brief, yet effective, Health and Safety Risk Assessment on Second Employee's Decorating: I know the red colour is terrible, but all I will say to you is that FINALLY Second Employee has painted over the Dark Purple Guest Room, and at least it is better than that. Indeed, both Esso and I are united in hoping that her Dark Purple Phase is now over, and, by implication, that some small improvement in her aesthetic sense is possible. Although I will also say, if I were Second Employee, I might have spent the money on a plasterer for the ceiling rather than just waving more more Johnstone's Vinyl Matt Emulsion at the situation and hoping for the best, but there we are. That's just me. What do I know.

Anyway, Larry, while I have been concentrating on Health and Safety, interior design consultancy (my advice to paint the room Ammonite ignored! like Cassandra!), almost 24/7 monitoring of BIRDIES and a forensic analysis of just what bulbs have survived Second Employee's very patchy understanding of Drainage and are managing to come up in our containers, what has Esso done? Well, first I asked him to monitor what podcasts Second Employee was listening to while she was painting her silly red colour, and he allowed her to listen to one about keeping chickens without even attempting to stop her! Well, Larry, if Second Employee manages to take leave of her senses to such an extent as to keep chickens when we have got absolutely no means of stopping them Wandering and causing trouble in Next Door's Garden and, frankly, potentially on quite a tricky and rather vital bit of the A6, then I am giving you notice now that I shall form them into a small Militia. No, Larry: I am afraid that morally I will be forced to do it. In fact, I do see some advantages to having a Small Chicken Militia, but even so I think Chickens will be bad for the Embassy; so I will put my own personal comfort and expansionist plans aside.

And the final insult, Larry, is that when I asked Esso to go and make sure Second Employee was not crocheting anything Ridiculous, because I really feel we need to move towards maintaining an Embassy which does not have Granny Squares in it in any capacity, I found the following: Esso fast asleep next to her, on a Granny Square, cuddling the wool. Cuddling the wool! And I bet he hadn't even started the Grade 1 Disciplinary Procedure. I honestly do not know - I do not know *at all* - how I am supposed to maintain discipline in such circumstances. Even if I did have a Chicken Militia it would be difficult (although perhaps a tiny bit easier). I am going to speak to Esso about his commitment to his job tonight, Larry, in the Firmest Terms: and, in the meantime, you might want to put a note about my Vastly Superior Dedication and Delivery on my Personnel File, Larry, and then when the next available transfer to Derbyshire Dales does come up we'll certainly know who deserves it most!

**February 2023**

Larry and the Catinet, this is Esso, Ambassador to the High Peak, with my update. Larry, Ghost staged an intervention on me the other night. She waited until I got up from a short rest of only about 10 or so hours on the back of the Downstairs Sofa, then she batted my tail with her paw, jumped on me, and said, Esso, you are turning into a Giant Lazy Arse and I am not having it. There is a Strategic Plan to deliver, the only one who has been doing any BIRDIE monitoring or Striding About Purposefully for a good few weeks is ME, we are behind on the Gantt Chart, and it is all categorically your fault.

So I had to break Employee Confidentiality, Larry, which I really feel terrible about. I said, Ghost, you are wrong. I have not been BIRDIE monitoring or Striding *solely* because I have been employed elsewhere. Second Employee has not been well, and I have been helping her; I have been delivering on the part of the Strategic Plan which states we should be Solid Furry Reassuring Presences where necessary. Larry, as I remember you observed yourself that time, one can say many things about Ghost: but her being a Solid Furry Reassuring Presence is not one of them, wonderful though her other qualities are. So, if anyone is going to be Solid and Furry, it has got to be me.

Anyway she said, what nonsense, Esso, there is nothing wrong with Second Employee anyway, and I had to say, look Ghost, she is suffering quite badly from Anxiety.

Well, you can imagine her reaction. She said, well, Esso, I would have Anxiety as well if I made as many Bad Choices as Second Employee does, in fact, it's a wonder the rest of us don't have Anxiety waiting for her to paint something else purple or perhaps drag home a scale replica of the Taj Mahal in papier mâché from the Cancer Research shop. Anyway, she's only got Anxiety because she thinks it's fashionable. Tell her it's actually fashionable to deliver on her KPIs without FUSSING and to introduce a few cool neutrals into rooms and then perhaps we'll get somewhere.

So I had to say, Ghost, she really does have Anxiety, her OCD has flared up quite badly and she's having trouble dealing with it. Ghost SNORTED, and said, OCD! And I bet it's not the useful kind where they clean things, is it, Esso, and I had to say, no, it's more the checking kind, and Larry, this nearly finished Ghost off. She said, well Esso, what is *even* the *point* of Second Employee checking anything when she never does it properly and she KNOWS I do the 6:30am PATROL every day without fail; even round the back of the freezer. Honestly, Esso, if it was left to you or Second Employee checking then neither of you would know when Mr Whiskers from Lightwood Road had been here at 3am nosing round our kickboards, the sneaky snake, and when you needed to pee on the books on the bottom shelf in the dining room to show him what's what. Esso, the arrogance of it, I am cross with Second Employee and I am cross with you. And with that she went upstairs to sit under her radiator.

So I really felt, Larry, that the conversation had not gone well, and indeed that my attempts to educate Ghost in line with the High Peak Embassy Mental Health Strategy 23-24 had been almost counterproductive; and I felt rather sad. But, later that evening, I went upstairs to talk to Ghost again, and I saw her sitting with Second Employee, purring, and licking her very carefully, saying, well, Second Employee, you're a terrible scruff but luckily you've got me here to do Competent Grooming so you shouldn't worry about things, everything is fine and I'm here to sort you out.

So, I slunk back downstairs quietly, and left them to it. I do think Ghost is trying to be supportive in her own way, Larry, and in the meantime Second Employee and I sit together on the Downstairs Sofa and drink coffee and read books and try to be calm, and soon it will be Spring even in the High Peak!

## February 2023

Larry and the Catinet. This is Ghost, Ambassador to the High Peak, with an Update combined with Helpful Advice to those of you who are Employers. As I believe Esso let you know last time, Second Employee has recently been even more RIDICULOUS than normal, trying to get out of Hard Work by pretending to 'have anxiety': and so Esso and I have been having lots of discussions about how to deal with the situation.

Obviously I suggested we invoke the Capability Procedure immediately, but unfortunately Esso thinks he is FOND of Second Employee and refuses to sack her; which is a continuing source of irritation to me. Anyway, after a full and frank discussion, Esso said he thought she would be better if she had something specific to focus on, rather than just Generalised Existential Dread, which does not, apparently, encourage an Employee to be more efficient in their duties. I don't know why it doesn't, but there we are, apparently that is the case.

Well, I thought giving Second Employee a proper focus was an excellent idea. For example, I have got a number of back issues of How To Be A Better Employee magazine which I really do not think Second Employee has read properly, so I thought *initially* we could lock her in a room with those and see what happens. But, it appeared that Esso had already - already, without discussing it with me first - given Second Employee permission to buy Yet More Bloody Yarn to crochet a Particularly Silly Blanket, and she has been industriously Beavering Away, and she has created a mad-looking square, which apparently she is going to continue crocheting on until it is blanket-sized. Larry, I will WhatsApp you a photo, and I would advise you to be sitting down when you open it, because I imagine you and I will be entirely united in our opinion of the aesthetic merits of this UTTER HORROR.

So, here is my helpful advice. Second Employee is not a bright employee, all Esso's NONSENSE about her being his Best Friend notwithstanding. She is a dim, suggestible, and credulous Employee. It is, therefore, very, very unfortunate that she has seen the creation of other Employees which are sometimes shared on Facebook. It was sadly predictable that Second Employee, having none of the innate taste of these other Employees, should look at other crocheted blanket creations, decide crochet is 'where it's at', and produce her own appalling silliness. There is no need to worry, though, Larry: I shall deal with it. I am allowing her to sit and FIDDLE with it for the moment, but, when it is complete, a judicious application of Claws and Teeth will ensure it unravels strategically and cannot be used.

However. What I think the Catinet may not realise is, when we allow our Employees to type our updates, they are able to read what we say, and the responses thereto: and can be influenced THUS by other Employees. This MONSTROSITY can at least serve as a Useful Warning of what can happen with Employee Collaboration! Can you imagine what else could develop? If we let this continue, they might form a union!

So I have taken steps. Firstly, I am typing this update myself. It takes me a little bit longer than Second Employee, who has very, very slightly longer fingers, but with practice and a fair wind I should be much quicker next time. Secondly, I have Tasked Esso with finding out how to change the password on Second Employee's laptop, because it seems to me that a lot of her Silly Ideas come from there; and also, if she does not have a laptop, she cannot Eavesdrop on the Catinet. I think these two firm, decisive actions will make a massive difference, and I advise all the other members of the Catinet to do the same with their own Employees.

Esso says that actually the reason Second Employee is crocheting something so SILLY is because 'she hasn't quite worked out how to crochet into a long chain, Ghost, if she could do that she might be able to make something more sensible': but I am not going to lower myself to discuss technicalities like that, and frankly I think Esso already knows too much. I am actually extremely worried he is going to start having opinions on Back Post Double Trebles, because then where shall we be! I am trying to keep us all on an even keel,

Larry, but I must confess that at the moment it is slightly hard work!

# Chapter 3
# Spring 2023: Tea and Tornadoes

**March 2023**

Larry and the Catinet. This is Esso, Joint Ambassador to the High Peak, with my update. Larry, the weather here has been challenging; but, luckily, I remembered a rather smart beanbag on the top floor and decided to sit it out there, which turned out to be an excellent strategy. Ghost said, go away, Esso, this is my floor, but Ghost has never sat on that beanbag as long as anyone has ever been able to remember so I said to her, Ghost you are being a Dog In The Manger again, and I took no notice. I know it sounds cruel, Larry, but I think sometimes with Ghost the best approach is to be Firm and Robust. For example, this week I am afraid I have had to be a little sharp with her. At the height of the weather difficulties, in the middle of a blizzard and when the Employees were completely snowed in and a little fractious, I was dozing comfortably on my beanbag when I hear a lot of FAFFING and COMMOTION, far away on the bottom floor.

Well, I thought nothing of it. I thought, probably Second Employee has just decided to either spray the kitchen orange or paint a pentagram on the tiles as instructed by this month's edition of Country Living, and First Employee is trying to dissuade her, or something of that ilk. Anyway, there was lots of running up and down stairs and raised voices, and then finally Second Employee shouted something triumphantly, and both the Employees started laughing.

Well, Ghost came running upstairs and said to me, Esso, where are the Health and Safety and Safeguarding Policies, because I am going to update both of them URGENTLY. Larry, I am afraid my heart sank. I said to her, what have you done, Ghost, and she was most indignant. But I probed, Larry, and it turned out that she had peed on the toaster, shorted all the electrics on the bottom two floors, and was angry that the Employees had LAUGHED and weren't grateful for her - and I quote - 'diligent safeguarding against Mr Whiskers from Lightwood Road coming in and sniffing round our freezer again'.

Well. Larry. I had to say to her, firstly there is currently over a foot of snow surrounding us in every direction and if Mr Whiskers wants to wade through that just to sniff round our freezer then, frankly, I think he can fill his boots: and also, you cannot just go shorting electrics willy nilly. What if you cause a fire in this weather, to start with they will never get a fire engine through, and also everyone will think it is hilarious and you will end up on the local news as The Cat Who Peed On The Toaster And Burnt Down An Entire Terrace Of Heavy Stone Houses

Which Had Stood Unmolested Since 1874. Ghost said, well, Esso, you may say that, but the Employees laughed at me, and I cannot put up with this level of Disrespect. It is almost as bad as when Second Employee picks me up, kisses my head, and says, I love you, tiny mad creature.

Well, Larry, I felt this was the right moment to have the discussion: I felt Ghost needed to be given a wake-up call. I said, look, Ghost, you may not like the Employees, but they are good natured and kind to us. I don't like to worry you, Ghost, but there are lots of Employees in this world who are not kind to Ambassadors; and perhaps you should reconcile yourself to the ones you have got, because they may not be perfect but they love you. Because, I said, warming to my theme, your main gripes with Second Employee really are that she has got no taste - which I agree she hasn't - and that she is dim. Well, Ghost, she is not dim, she has actually got qualifications.

Larry, this was probably the wrong thing to say, because Ghost gave me a rather old-fashioned look and said, yes, Esso, but are they useful qualifications? And I had to confess that they were not. In fact, I wished I hadn't mentioned it. But luckily Ghost became otherwise preoccupied, and she said, why would Employees not be kind, Esso, I don't believe you. Well, I did not like to press my point, Larry, because I know Ghost worries: and anyway, the next day First Employee told her the weather had been 'enough to make anyone pee on a toaster' which made her feel better, because I suspect by that point she realised that her Safeguarding had been a little misjudged: and then she decided to write a Second Employee Training Strategy so she can 'address Second Employee's Skills Gap head on and sort things out'.

So, Larry, all is well. The snow has melted, and although there *was* a small tornado this morning, it was at least down the road and not in our back garden: and we are all happy again. I did see Second Employee earlier looking at some crochet patterns on her laptop which Ghost really, really, really will not approve of: but, Larry, I shall save that conversation for another day!

## March 2023

Larry, and the Catinet. This is Esso, Ambassador to the High Peak and Minister for Aesthetic Standards (temporary), with my report. Larry, you will notice that I have given myself a Ministry there. I do hope you don't mind. It's just for the time being. I shall give up my title soon. I've only done it, frankly, to pull rank with Ghost, because she's caused such an Unholy Fuss over poor Second Employee and her Crochet Thing that I've decided it's the best way to put an end to it. So I I pretended you'd appointed me, and I'm hoping it will shut her up, just for a few weeks, if she thinks I have the final say.

I said to her, yes, Ghost, that's me, New Minister for Aesthetic Standards with a Special Interest in Handicrafts, and so if I say Second Employee can carry on fiddling about with her crochet then she can. And I must say, Larry, since I've been Minister for Aesthetic Standards, I've found it rather interesting. For instance, I said to Ghost, look, Ghost, I've realised the dresser downstairs is grey, look at that, why doesn't that meet your requirements for minimalism. Because I honestly can't see any reason why it wouldn't. And also Second Employee has had the lights taken out in our sitting room and replaced them with some funny paper ones, which are white. Well, why isn't white minimalist? Of course it is. So now, Ghost, we've got a minimalist kitchen and a minimalist sitting room, both identified by me, Minister for Aesthetic Standards, and you can stop moaning.

Well, Larry, this will astonish you just like it did me; but Ghost wasn't satisfied with that. She said, Esso, if you think either of those things are minimalist and tasteful then I literally don't know what to say to you, and frankly I shall just sit here silently with my eyes closed from now on and think of Le Corbusier. Although, before I withdraw entirely into judgemental silence, I shall just say, why has Second Employee taken out perfectly sensible chandeliers anyway and replaced them with mad £10 things from Ikea, who even does that, frankly it is as if she is mocking me; and not only that, but I also had to sit and listen to her having that tortured conversation with the electrician about whether she wanted a 6 inch or a 9 inch pendant and then she chose the one he hadn't got in his van, and made him drive to B&Q even though the traffic lights were out at the junction at the bottom of the High Street near the Dog Café and it was literal carnage. These are the consequences, Esso, of Second Employee and her lack of taste, and if the Catinet think you, rather than I who actually understand Muted Colour Palettes, can take that on, then I say *good luck to all of you*. And with that she flounced off to go and sit under her radiator.

Well, Larry, of course I defend Second Employee to Ghost: but she did put on an Afternoon Tea for her mother last Sunday at which she wore the most astonishing creation. It is difficult to describe, but it seemed to feature both pink frills and pictures of Elvis in the same garment. I did hear her mother saying, wasn't it nice that Second Employee wasn't constrained by fashion or what other people thought. Second Employee seemed perfectly happy with that, because she says it is true and she isn't constrained by either: but Ghost gave me a very pointed look, which I studiously ignored.

Larry, I do understand that Second Employee probably isn't Quite The Thing: but we are very good friends, and I really would like to keep her, if possible. Also, and I know you will keep this strictly confidential, but I have found myself growing rather interested in Crochet. Second Employee and I sit and do it together. It took us a while to work out Crab Stitch, but we got there eventually. I think, Larry, whatever Ghost says, it is good for Ambassadors to have a creative outlet, and perhaps, frankly, if she would only take up Macramé or perhaps Weaving On A Peg Loom she wouldn't be so jolly negative all the time!

**March 2023**

Larry, this is Ghost, and I do not know what nonsense we are having here about certain cats being Ministers For Aesthetic Standards. If anyone was *actually* Minister For Aesthetic Standards and they walked into this Embassy, I *personally* think they would spontaneously combust with horror.

Also, Larry, I have added to the Strategic Plan the directive that Second Employee should not be allowed to wear her Elvis dress in public, even if that public is only her family, because it does not do the dignity of the Embassy any good to have her looked at askance and damned with faint praise, and also I cannot think of one sensible reason why she is not able to identify and purchase something sensible and relatively flattering in viscose, like a normal person. Let me emphasis that: not one sensible reason. She presumably has access to the same shops and websites as the rest of the country.

Also, Esso has asked me if I feel I would be more cheerful if I took up Weaving On A Peg Loom: I would not, Larry. Not unless, perhaps, I wove straps with which to tie up all the doors of the Embassy, with Esso and the Employees on the other side while I got Competent Men In to paint everywhere Ammonite and give us a fresh start. Or generally to tie up Second Employee to stop her interfering with Proceedings. I am fairly confident that that is the *only situation* in which a Peg Loom could possibly improve my mood!

**March 2023**

Larry, this is Esso, Ambassador to the High Peak and Minister for Aesthetic Standards, with an update. Larry, it is still rather cold here. I don't know if it is Spring yet where you are, but we in Buxton are still having quite challenging weather. Second Employee says we have got to keep the faith and that even in Buxton spring comes eventually, it is just that it is usually a month later than everywhere else. I must say, I am looking forward to the two weeks in July when sometimes it doesn't rain all the time. I have made a list of all the things I am going to do:

1/ Watch the Birdies. Graham next door has really been enormously kind and has set up a Birdie Feeding Station, which attracts all sorts of Interesting Feathered Creatures who Chirrup and Fly About in terribly attractive ways. Ghost and I mostly just watch, really mostly just watch and that is all we do. Mostly.

Besides, when we very, very occasionally take Small Birdies into the Embassy to play a special game with, First Employee insists on joining in the game and wraps them up in a tea towel and relocates them saying, Mr Esso Puss Puss Cat, no more Birdies In This House. And honestly I do love First Employee, but that makes it less fun.

2/ Lie on the garden in the sun with my Leggies in the air. In the meantime, I am lying near radiators, on the back of the Downstairs Sofa, or on the Spare Room Bed in the same position, so I can practise.

3/ Stay out all night watching the drug dealer and making friends with his clients. They are so lovely! They say, aren't you a friendly cat, and they stroke me, and of course I do not like to make comparisons with Second Employee's Mother in terms of Politeness and Innate Courtesy but they do not mention my teeth once.

4/ Chase Ghost up and down the steps down to the back garden. Ghost says the Strategic Plan Appendix J Health And Safety forbids Stair Chasey when they are slippy from rain, sleet, hail, or ice, which is 95% of the year: but in the two weeks in July when it is sunny the Stair Chasey Tournament is really fabulous fun. Sometimes Mr Chunky Half Tail Black Cat joins in too; he is very keen but I think he can be a little inelegant.

5/ Go and sit in the patch of grass next to the Jitty, get entirely covered in seeds, and then go back in the house and avoid Second Employee who says, Mr Esso let me brush your seeds off they are driving me mad looking at you. It's a great game and has the bonus of getting some steps in for Second Employee, which is good for her.

So you see, Larry, even though at the moment it feels like Spring will never come, soon it will be here, then lovely summer, then the happy cold times again, and finally the Festival Of Cat Toys Tied To A Tree. So may happy times to come! I I know Ghost says differently, but we really are extremely lucky cats!

[Note from Esso: I have been told that a Jitty is not called a Jitty in all parts of the country, so it is possible that this part of my update may be a little unclear. All I can say to that is, if it is not called a Jitty, it should be. That is what it is! Goodness me.]

## April 2023

Larry and the Catinet. This is Ghost, Ambassador to the High Peak and Shadow Minister for Aesthetic Standards. Larry, firstly I would like to say to you once more, I do not know why Esso says he has been made Minister for Aesthetic Standards and I am merely the Shadow Minister, because not only does Esso even look like a Shadow, but, he tried to suggest to me the other day that our kitchen dresser is actually minimalist and tasteful 'because it is grey' and that I should 'stop going on'.

Larry, I am WhatsApping you a picture of said Dresser, which contains all the mad pointless brightly coloured objects Second Employee has been able to find in a two thousand mile radius of Buxton and arrange with no THOUGHT of either Aesthetic Balance or Sense. I imagine when you have looked at it and you have FINISHED LAUGHING at the thought of this being minimalist and tasteful, you will want to IMMEDIATELY STRIP Esso of his Ministry, and then probably BOOP him on the nose to emphasise the point.

Esso said to me, don't question things Ghost, of course Larry knows best: so of course I am not questioning anything. I am just remarking in an utterly disinterested and entirely professional manner that Esso being Minister for Aesthetic Standards is Completely and Utterly Ridiculous, and that he would not know Clean Lines or Cool Neutrals if they collectively chased him off his sofa and bit him on the bum!

Anyway. I spent today, Larry, resting on the Guest Room Bed, thinking that you would be able to see a rather nice view out of the window if the double glazing had not got condensation in between the layers. I have told the Employees time and time again that they need to get all the windows resealed. Esso says they have probably not got enough money to do it, which is further evidence, Larry, that the Employees make Bad Choices, and spend the tiny amount of money I imagine it would cost to replace four storeys' worth of bay windows on silly things like Cake.

Never mind. Some day a reckoning will come. Besides, today in my update I would like to focus on making a Minor Yet Important Complaint about something very Silly which First Employee has done. Because, Larry, First Employee managed to fall out with the man who Originally Redid Our Outside Steps over the comparative desirability of bringing concrete up our back lane in a lorry versus mixing it slowly and ineffectually in a bucket with a teaspoon, a situation in which I must confess a certain sneaking sympathy for First Employee, our outside steps have ended up *a little bit quirky*; and are therefore not very safe for Employees to go up and down in the dark, especially since they are covered in Black Ice for six months of the year.

So, First Employee has been waging an ineffectual War of Outside Illumination since last October, which has involved buying various outside lights and installing them at strategic points around the most dangerous parts of our back garden; and finally, as a triumphant Final Blow, he has stuck a motion-sensitive one just above our back door. This is annoying, Larry, because every time I LEAP through the back catflap at night I trigger it, and really most of the time I am going out to do things which I do not want to draw attention to; and yet it is so bright it alerts the whole neighbourhood. Indeed, Mr Chunky Half Tail Black Cat said to me the other evening, look at you, Ghost, leaping through into the spotlight like a Hairy Norma Desmond: and Larry, I will not have Mr Chunky saying such things, however accurate they might be, so if you could have a word with First Employee that would be good. Thank you.

Also, Second Employee wandered home the other day with a Very Silly Plant which she has installed on top of the Ceramic Elephant, saying someone 'gave it to her'. What kind of life, Larry, does Second Employee lead which involves people randomly thrusting Spider Plants at her at the first opportunity? The wrong kind of life, that is the answer. Esso said, oh look, Ghost, let her be with her spider plant, what harm is it doing: but I am concerned, Larry, that Second Employee is attempting, however incompetently, to establish a Primitive Barter Economy. If I believe it is likely to progress to a point where it threatens GDP, I shall make sure to let you know. The establishment of inferior economic systems by Employees is not part, as far as I am aware, of the High Peak Strategic Plan 23-24: and some of us still care about delivering the Strategic Plan: even though we might only be Shadow Ministers!

## April 2023

Larry and the Catinet: this is Esso, Ambassador to the High Peak and Minister for Aesthetic Standards. Larry, something very sad has happened: Grey Next Door Cat's Employee has passed into the Afterwards, and Grey Next Door Cat is going to go and live with other Employees. We had a long chat about it the other day. He told me he was going to live with his Employee's son and his family, in a 'lovely big semi in Dovedale with a secure garden'.

I said how nice that sounded: and then he said something to me that didn't worry me at all. Not even a little bit. I mean, I really can barely remember it even enough to report it. Really I am going to have to think carefully! Anyway I *think* he said, 'well, Esso, I'm a lovely colour that's very fashionable at the moment, so I had a lot of Employees wanting to take me on: I don't imagine you'd have the same. No-one ever wants black cats, do they? I don't know where you'd end up if your Employees didn't want you any more'.

Larry, I didn't say anything, and in fact we're making plans at the North Buxton Monochrome Cat Alliance to visit when he's properly settled in. I spent all yesterday evening curled up on Second Employee's lap, purring, and she said, Mr Esso look at your lovely thick black fur, it's just like an expensive velvet coat!

**April 2023**

Larry and the Catinet. This is Esso, Ambassador to the High Peak and Minister for Aesthetic Standards, with a really extremely worrying update! Larry, Second Employee has gone quite mad! The Employees are in Spain at the moment, making First Employee's House into an AirBnB, and they were supposed to be staying in it as well: but Larry, the day before they left, Second Employee burst into tears, put her head in her hands, and said she *hated that bloody house* and if she had got to stay in it again she was refusing to *even get on the plane.*

Larry! After all that work I have done with Second Employee about knowing our Duty, and carrying it out whatever the personal cost! And then, Larry, it got worse. Because Second Employee was being difficult, the Employees had to book an apartment on the coast instead: and the one they found was almost entirely grey, and the bits that were not grey were white and shiny. It is in a place where even the sand is grey! Larry, this is everything Second Employee and I stand united against: but she said, whenever she thinks of First Employee's Spanish House, she feels she never wants to see a quirky house with character ever again and actually what she wants is to sit for a week somewhere 'grey and faceless and liminal'.

Well, you can imagine what Ghost has said about this, Larry. I was hoping she would not CROW and EXULT, but I am afraid I hoped in vain, and she said to me, look, Esso, this is what happens with your Minister for Aesthetic Standards Nonsense, and in fact as soon as you have taken over with your Silly Ministry which I strongly suspect is Utterly Made Up, then Second Employee has done a Volte Face so profound that I frankly think it is a testament to your Utter Incompetence in the role. Larry, it really is a terrible development. I had been looking at crochet patterns online and I found one which I really thought Second Employee would enjoy making when she comes back on Saturday, and also I was thinking we could restart our mosaic work and perhaps makeover a small plant stand. I had so many ideas for Second Employee, and perhaps they are all in vain!

I do hope, Larry, she manages to find some lovely tiles, or something nice and bright, even on the coast, and remembers our Aesthetic Standards. Ghost keeps walking past me and SMIRKING, and I really am finding it difficult to bear. Interim Summer Employee is here carrying out the necessary duties, and I have been trying to continue with his Martial Arts Training in which he was making so much progress, but, honestly, my heart isn't in it, and nor even are my teeth. I shall keep you updated, Larry, with developments, when the Employees return: but Ghost is already pressurising me to buy a job lot of Ammonite Emulsion so that 'Second Employee can crack straight on with things when she gets back now she is finally sensible', and I am finding it rather hard to stay cheerful!

## April 2023

Larry and the Catinet. This is Ghost, Ambassador to the High Peak and Shadow Minister for Aesthetic Standards here with my report. Well, Larry, the Prodigals have Returned from being RIDICULOUS on the Costa Del Sol. They are covered in mosquito bites, which is something that happens SOLELY to Employees who are Morally Weak. I said to Esso, don't you go implying to either of the Employees that we've missed them even a little bit; but I've seen him following Second Employee round and trilling and purring, and nuzzling her with his head. There's no wonder I have such trouble maintaining my Elevated Employee Behavioural Standards. Larry, Second Employee said to me, look Ghost, here I am back just when I said I would be: but I *personally* heard her telling Esso that they'd nearly missed the plane in Malaga because they'd been FAFFING ABOUT in Costa eating a chocolate croissant, and by the time they realised what time it was it was Last Call For Boarding. And First Employee had to have his bag searched because he'd not separated out the toothpaste, and the Customs Agent found his Special Fig Sausage which he buys from the local shop, and laughed.

So I do not, frankly, think the Employees have done anything at all to improve Spanish - UK relations, going wandering about finding a Costa when they should only drink authentic Spanish espresso to start with, and hiding comedy sausages in their luggage; and so I have decided to impound their passports until such time as they can prove to me they can be trusted. Frankly, Larry, I feel that will be never.

Anyway, Larry, apparently the Employees are very pleased with themselves, because they have managed to 'sort the Spanish house out' and it will be ready to go on Airbnb as soon as they have sorted out the paperwork. Second Employee has shown me a photograph of it and said, look, Ghostycat, you can see why I do not want to deal with anything authentic ever again, I have embraced my inner shallows and the next time I go to Spain I shall spend the entire time either in a Beach Bar eating grilled sardines and looking at the sea from a safe distance, or drinking café con leche no more than ten paces from a ceramics shop.

Well, Larry, I do not think Second Employee's inner shallows have ever been particularly well hidden: I personally have always found her an exceptionally facile Employee. I also do not think, having seen the photograph, that there is anything at all about that house that could conceivably create practical problems; even if it is right at the top of a mountain with Mountain Goats and Ibex wandering about, as Second Employee says it is. What could possibly be difficult about having spent many holidays manoeuvring a king size mattress up a spiral staircase or thirty boxes of books down one, or putting together 'an enormous amount of IKEA furniture' in forty degree heat with no air conditioning? I think it is only her Moral Weakness, which I alluded to previously, which makes it challenging.

I actually feel, if I was there, I would have dealt with things much better: firstly, I might have Organised the Goats, particularly, in a slightly more structured way. In fact, I wonder if I have been not ambitious enough with my plans for the Small Chicken Militia: perhaps I should have a Small Goat Militia instead. I really feel that is something with which one could achieve a great deal! Larry, perhaps you could tell me your thoughts on the desirability of my establishing an Iberian Goat Militia, and, in the meantime, I can see if Esso bought that job lot of Ammonite Paint like I told him to so I can get Second Employee to work before she changes her mind!

[Note from Ghost: I find it very painful to look back and see my Dreams for the Goat Militia and contrast it with the present reality. It is a good job I am unusually emotionally robust. It really is.]

## May 2023

Larry and the Catinet. This is Ghost, Ambassador to the High Peak and Shadow Minister for Aesthetic Standards, with a Very Serious Complaint. Larry, Esso has been difficult. We have had to have WORDS. It began the other morning, when I was catching up on some sleep on the suitcase on top of the wardrobe. I find, Larry, if I am asleep on the suitcase on top of the wardrobe, then, if Second Employee were to try, for example, to pack things into it to go and be Utterly Ridiculous in Spain for weeks and weeks and weeks leaving me all on my own without anyone to love me or stroke me at all or tell me how soft I am, then I would know: and I would be able to stop her. So it is a particularly sensible action to take which aligns perfectly with my KPIs, and if Esso wasn't Slightly Too Chunky to get up on top of the wardrobe then I am sure he would do it too.

Anyway, I was fast asleep, having a rather disquieting dream about losing control of the Potential Small Goat Militia and them forming an Unhelpful Goat Union and making speeches: when I heard Second Employee saying, well I don't know where she is, I shall look in here One Last Time. Then she came STOMPING IN, waking me up, and I shouted, BRRRRRRRRRPPP, Second Employee keep it down, some of us are trying to sleep in here. Second Employee saw me and seemed surprised and said, Ghostycat where have you been, I've been looking all over for you, you Sneaky Animal!

Well, Larry, obviously I am deeply insulted. I discussed it with Esso afterwards and he said not to take any notice, because he thought perhaps Second Employee was a little bit tired because she had been up from the basement to the top floor three times looking for me; and since she is finally appreciating the Negative Effects Of Cake she has been out running four times this week and perhaps didn't enjoy doing all those stairs. Esso said, moreover, although it is a little bit rude, if we look at it in *strictly technical* terms then we are animals, just like the Employees are; although, of course, we are much more noble animals than them.

Well, Larry, of course Esso is right: and all I said was, well, we might be animals, or, if we think about Granny on our Mother's Side who was at least Half Demon, we might possibly be at least partly Small House Demons as well. That is all I said. And it is true. And Larry, I think Second Employee has understood this anyway, because I heard her only last week saying to First Employee that she 'felt much better about the cat situation now she realised they weren't pets at all but small demons who live in the same house': so, although I never entirely feel Second Employee is entirely Au Fait with the small print of her Employment Contract, at least on the Demon Question I feel we are on the same page.

Well, Larry, Esso really caused a FUSS. He said, I have told you, Ghost, we are not Small House Demons and we are going to forget entirely about Granny On Our Mother's Side. We are Professional Ambassadors with a Strategic Plan which has Appendices and a Risk Register and it does not get more corporate and above board than that. Then, Larry, he looked at me beadily and he said, also, Ghost, I hope you are not doing any of the things that Granny On Our Mother's Side taught you, for instance, I hope you really *were* asleep on the suitcase when Second Employee was stomping up and down the stairs panicking, and not IN FACT doing your Disappearing and Appearing In Surprising Places.

Well, Larry, I actually was not. I was asleep, worrying about the Goats, because I am the only one in this family who takes proper responsibility for things. But, theoretically: if, very occasionally, one wanted to make use a of a fairly anodyne trick taught to one by a beloved family member, I don't think that would be a problem, would it? Because there really are a lot of stairs in this house, and when I am on the top floor and I hear Second Employee Being Very Silly In The Basement, I need to get down there instantly to stop her: and if I know a good way to do that - well. I think if no-one asks, I will perhaps not say anything. So forget I mentioned it, Larry, and I shall go and make friends with Esso again and just ask him if he can remember how to Summon Things, like Granny taught him!

P.S. Second Employee has wandered home tonight with something very strange in a jar which she says someone gave her and which she is calling a 'kefir starter'. I cannot see how this can lead to anything good: I shall ask Esso to add an appendix to the Strategic Plan to stop Second Employee wandering off and being given silly things, because this keeps happening; and in the short term I shall see if I can knock it off the dresser.

## May 2023

Larry and the Catinet. This is Esso, Minister for Aesthetic Standards and Ambassador to the High Peak, with a brief update. Larry, Second Employee has asked if, as a special dispensation, I can notify the Employees of the Catinet about her progress on her Crochet, and I have granted permission. She has created a rather surprising-looking circular colourful mandala-type thing which I understand is 'supposed to turn into a throw' (Ghost says she would certainly like to throw it somewhere, possibly from off the top of Mam Tor). She is not very far along because she is not a quick crocheter, and also because 'people keep making her go and suffer up Spanish mountains for weeks'; but nevertheless, I like to encourage her. I feel it is a wholesome hobby.

Ghost said, I hope you are not COLLUDING in Second Employee's NONSENSE, Esso, but I said, well I may be, Ghost, but then who is it who has been telling everybody about Granny On Our Mother's Side when we AGREED we would keep her Demonic Nature a secret now we are Professionals, and she had no answer to that. It is very rare Ghost has no answer to anything, so I have taken advantage of the brief moment.

Also, Larry, despite Ghost having waged an email campaign ever since she found out about it, there has been a Wool Fair today just down the road. This appears to be a thing where a lot of Employees all go into a room and become overexcited, and spend money they do not have on very brightly coloured WOOL for their Employers to toss around rooms, which I think is fun; but of course Ghost thinks is very silly. Second Employee has come back from there with no WOOL, which is rather remiss, although I suppose we do have some to be going on with; but with something called 'procion dyes', which she is going to use to 'tie dye something or other'.

I have not heard of this before, Larry - it's a new one on me. Ghost says if it's something Second Employee is thinking of doing then it's 'bound to be appalling, frankly' and she 'might as well just go and live in a hedge because at least then there won't be this continual assault on the senses': but I think, Larry, Ghost is just being GRUMPY because Second Employee's Family are coming tomorrow, and last time Second Employee's Mother was here she said I was 'a really exceptionally beautiful cat'. Ghost says, don't listen, Esso, she's just trying to get round you so you don't bite her: but I think it is a real endorsement of my continued diplomatic efforts with Second Employee's Family (with the obvious disclaimer that I am not responsible for anything my teeth might do, now or in the future) that they can now appreciate my 'lovely thick black fur', although they are 'never quite sure what he is thinking' and they all say 'ooooooooh' nervously whenever I stretch my paws out. Well: mostly I am thinking about the Strategic Plan, and the challenges we still have in its delivery: but this evening I am having a brief rest from my endeavours because there is a lovely sun puddle next to the piano and I am on my back with all my LEGGIES in the air!

**May 2023**

Larry and the Catinet. This is Esso, Minister for Aesthetic Standards and Ambassador to the High Peak. Larry, could I ask you to bring to the attention of the Catinet the photograph of me I WhatsApped to you earlier: as I have occasionally detected a slight cynicism in certain quarters when I say, quite truthfully, that Ghost and I are exactly the same colour with only a very, very minor variation in the distribution of the white in our fur. I feel this photograph of my very beautiful coat which is actually a mix of colours shows extremely clearly quite how much white in my fur there is. Ghost said, for God's sake Esso, you have got literally less than 20 white hairs there and if you show them that photo they will all be able to count them for themselves and then no-one will listen to a word you say about anything afterwards, especially when you say, for example, Ghost that is my beanbag not yours, and I already don't listen to that.

Well, Larry, Ghost is overly cynical, as ever: I said nothing in response. I merely present this photo so the Catinet can see the fur situation, which is quite clear, for themselves. Also, Larry, I have a very, very major Diplomatic Success to report. It turns out that Second Employee's Father is having some Memory Challenges, and that he has forgotten about my teeth previously taking the action they may or may not have done with regards to him, which may or may not have led to a course of antibiotics: and to the Employees having to be immediately recalled from whatever nonsense they were doing in A Mousehole, from where they did not even bring me A Mouse. Although, could you please note for my file, that Second Employee's Father's subsequent visit to hospital was never *explicitly proven* to have a causal connection with the actions (or not) of my teeth.

Anyway, now Second Employee's Father and I are friends again! When he comes to visit Ghost and I, I sit on the newspaper he is reading and I PURR, and I NUDGE him with my head, and he strokes me and says, hello, Mr Pussycat, aren't you lovely: and Second Employee's Mother says very loudly, Paul for God's sake do not touch that cat, he is a very bad cat and he will bite you, do you not remember him biting you before, and Second Employee's Father says to her very clearly, No. I really cannot overstate to you, Larry, the joy this development gives me. It makes me feel that redemption is possible for all of us.

Ghost says, Esso, you cannot rely on people developing Memory Challenges as a get out of jail free card when you have bitten them, but of course I am not doing that! I am just remarking that clearly Second Employee's Father considers the incident so minor, as do I, that he has decided it is not worth filing in his short to medium term memory. Ghost says, is that really the case, Esso, because he seems to have also decided it is not worth remembering the fact that the Employees live in the Embassy, and one might have thought that was something worth keeping in mind, because otherwise frankly he must be continually wondering why people are making him visit a very tall house in the middle of nowhere which has been painted in inappropriate colours. But as I said to Ghost: that has already been explained perfectly satisfactorily by Second Employee's Brother, who said, look, Susie, it's all fine, Dad clearly just can't believe anyone would willingly have bought a house with quite so many stairs.

So now we often hear Second Employee saying cheerfully, yes dad, I do live here, UNLIKELY AS THAT MAY SEEM. It really is all working out very, very well, Larry. I *personally* would recommend Memory Challenges to everyone, although I do hope Second Employee never forgets I am her Precious Slinky Esso and her Special Best Friend.

Now if only Second Employee's Mother could be persuaded to forget her Lifelong Terror And Distrust of Cats (although Ghost says there is even less chance of that than of her forgetting when the Sutton In Ashfield Factory Shop does the Triple Discount on Cashmere Cardigans), imagine how well we could all get on!

**May 2023**

Larry and the Catinet, this is Ghost, Ambassador to the High Peak and Shadow Minister for Aesthetic Standards with my report. Larry, firstly I need to notify you that I've discovered a Portal To Hell in the bathroom on the top floor. Esso said, look Ghost, I know you've never liked that extractor fan, but that's all it is; do you think Second Employee would really let you sit there staring at it while she brushes her teeth every night if either of you were in any danger. Well, Larry, I've Put A Temporary Psychic Seal on it (staring! ha!) and I've now notified both you and Esso: so I'd like to state formally that I consider myself to have discharged my Disclosure Responsibility, and If Second Employee manages to Summon The Devil while she's faffing about with her dental floss then on your heads be it and more fool her. Because I can tell you for nothing that the last thing we need is the Devil stalking round Our Top Floor interfering with the beanbag and criticising the bedding choices, although I suppose he might finally slap a coat of Annie Sloan on that awful bookcase Second Employee's been saying she's going to 'upcycle' since April.

Also, Larry, Second Employee is on a health kick again. She is running four times a week, and she is reading a very silly book which suggests Employees should waste all their time cooking everything from scratch rather than putting a small item on a plastic tray in the microwave and then spending the time saved on stroking Employers and telling them how very, very soft and precious they are. Second Employee says she cannot understand how she can still put weight on despite making her own yoghurt and RUNNING and RUNNING all round Buxton, forming opinions on the attractiveness of people's front gardens. Well, Larry, I can certainly understand it, because all the RUNNING is doing is making her hungry, and then she comes home and bakes cake. In fact, Second Employee is currently trapped in a kind of Perpetual Motion Cycle, where she RUNS, makes cake, eats cake, and then RUNS again. I have said to Esso, somehow we have to work out a way to get Second Employee off this treadmill, but Esso says, oh let her be, Ghost, she'll move on to something else soon. However, I would like to put in a Formal Request, Larry, for Employee Retraining, because there seems to be no end to the ways they find of being Silly, and I think it is best to address this kind of thing through a Formal Structure.

And could I also request that a Law be Passed ASAP to stop First Employee calling me Mrs G, because although I am having trouble articulating exactly why, I feel it does not come from an appropriately deferential place. Thank you. Honestly, Larry, one day Esso and I will have trained the Employees sufficiently that we can really begin the hard work of Strategic Plan Delivery, and I can't tell you how eagerly I look forward to that day!

**May 2023**

Larry and the Catinet, this is Ghost. I have been PONDERING. Larry, why is it that when Ambassadors have really eminently sensible and perfectly descriptive names like Ghost, and Esso which is perhaps not quite as sensible as Ghost, do Employees want to give them new ones? Why is it that, as I have alluded to above, First Employee is always insisting on calling me Mrs G? Or, why does Second Employee pick Esso up, kiss his small black furry head, and say, look at you, Mr Esso Puss Puss Cat? Or, even more appallingly, Mr Cuddles? Even *worse*, why does First Employee sing the following song every time he sees me, which he has made up, but which I understand to be based on some nonsense about Eric The Bee by Monty Python:

Mrs G
Philosophically
Is Ipso Facto
Half Not-G!

I really have no patience with this kind of thing. What if I started doing the same thing with the Employees? What if every time I walked past Second Employee I said, look at you over there,

Dungarees: or, have you remembered to defrost the chicken, Dworkin? Or if when I saw First Employee I shouted, lovely weather, isn't it, Foghorn Voice? I imagine they would not like it. And yet Esso and I are expected to put up with worse. I consider it to be indicative of a profound, creeping Disrespect: and I shall think of ways to put a stop to it over the coming months.

[Note from Ghost: Esso says he actually loves being Mr Chunky Chonk and Mr Cuddles, and sees both of these ridiculous names of 'symbols of love and affection'. This is why we in the feline community have the troubles we have, Larry: too much willingness among a small but vocal minority to trade respect and dignity for LOVE. As Prince Charles once famously said: *whatever love is*.]

**May 2023**

Larry and the Catinet, this is Esso, Ambassador to the High Peak, and Minister for Aesthetic Standards. Larry, I have a couple of things to report which are all completely unrelated to each other and not connected at all. Firstly, and frankly this one is of so little importance I could barely remember it to include it in my update: First Employee's Sister has got a new kitten, who is ginger.

Obviously this has no relevance to, or implications for, my role at all: I only mention it in the spirit of specifying new connections, so that everyone can be aware in case there is ever a Conflict Of Interest. Ghost said, aren't you worried, Esso, what if Second Employee decides she'd rather be employed by a Nice Friendly Ginger Cat than you; and also what if he's had a better upbringing and didn't come from a Heroin Addict Via Chesterfield Cats' Protection and doesn't have the same issues with his Teeth taking action independently of his Better Judgement. Well, Ghost later clarified when I bit her on the bum that she was of course 'joking', so I don't think we need to update the Risk Register. Or, at least, I *have* updated the Risk Register, but I have specified that the risk of Second Employee deciding she would prefer a New Ginger Kitten to me is probably less than 15%, and although I have marked the cell on the spreadsheet in amber (in line with my Traffic Light System) as the risk is theoretically present, I have made it a very pale amber. (Not ginger, as Ghost said, which was apparently also a joke!)

The further things I would like to report, Larry, which are completely unconnected with my previous paragraph, are, firstly, that I have updated my CV. I thought it would be useful, just on the off-chance that anyone should ever come along and say, Esso, what do you bring to this household. I have added to the Special Skills section the following:

Very velvety fur in a variety of interesting colours (at least 2)

*Very* loud purr

Admirable determination to Build Bridges with Second Employee's Mother despite her Ongoing Silly Recalcitrance

Inspirational Leader in Finding Unusual Places To Sleep - I PIONEERED the top-floor beanbag, and am currently working on the spare-room rolled-up-rug which the Employees don't know what to do with

Equally skilled at Crochet, and Martial Arts. Have extensive experience of training Second Employee and Interim Summer Employee in these respectively.

I think these additions make my CV particularly impressive, Larry. I obviously don't like to make comparisons, but there are probably some other cats who can only really put 'being ginger' in the Special Skills section, and who, moreover, think that is sufficient. I find that rather sad.

Anyway, the final thing I would like to add is that I have been looking through the Online Employee Training Manual, and I would like to register Second Employee for the following courses: *Appreciating the Beauty of Black Cats*, and, *How Not To Be Influenced By Family Members*. Ghost has pointed out that Second Employee DID NOT REST until she had got a very silly spiky 'acupressure' mat after Interim Summer Employee had got one; and although Ghost has attempted a number of times to walk across it, it is not comfortable for Ambassadors, and was therefore a very silly purchase. So we think the second course is particularly urgent; as Second Employee has form. If you could set everything up and email me the Zoom links, Larry, I will see she attends both of them, and even does the multiple choice at the end! Thank you Larry, and I'll update again soon.

# Chapter 4
# Summer 2023: Sausage Rolls and Spain

**June 2023**

Larry, this is Esso, Ambassador to the High Peak and Minister For Aesthetic Standards. Larry, I just wanted to state categorically for the benefit of those Employees who are still, dare I say, a little cynical about my very complex colouring; a Shaft Of Light shone on me earlier, and revealed me to be actually brown. I shall leave everyone to process this new information, Larry, and I shall continue to have a Nice Lie Down while I consider how much of the Strategic Plan will need to be rewritten in the light of this.

What price ginger kittens now, Larry!

**June 2023**

Larry, and the Catinet, this is Ghost, Ambassador to the High Peak and Shadow Minister for Aesthetic Standards, with my report. Firstly, Larry, I would like to notify you that I have banned Petunias. Second Employee keeps wandering home with particularly egregious-looking purple ones from Aldi which 'look cheerful', and Larry, they really are terribly common.

Esso said, come on Ghost, don't be all Phone For The Fish Knives, Norman, Second Employee can be common if she wants to be and besides I rather like them. Well, Larry, I don't know what Esso is muttering about or who Norman is, but I imagine he likes Petunias, which I do not, so I have banned them; and Second Employee can think about what flowers she would have in pots if she was a Proper Employee who wore deconstructed grey linen, and go and purchase those.

Secondly, there has been a very minor issue but fortunately it's all sorted out now. I've been elected Vice Chair of the North Buxton Monochrome Cat Alliance, and of course my first action in post was to expel Esso because now he identifies as brown he isn't monochrome any more. So that was Esso's fault. Now, at the first meeting, I may *possibly* have said something *very slightly unwise*, but in my defence I was very annoyed with Second Employee that day; because she has made a Very Silly Blackboard in the kitchen, and not one single one of the Employees or their Associates has thought of anything sensible to put on it yet. In fact, most of it is lyrics which Second Employee writes down from the Silly Songs she listens to when she is cooking, or ridiculous thoughts she has, or ridiculous QUOTES she has remembered. What use is such a thing?! At least if she wrote her KPIs on it it might keep them in the Forefront of her Mind.

Anyway, all I said was that I was *absolutely sick* of living in the Embassy with Silly Employees, and if anyone wanted to come and live there instead they were very welcome because frankly I would be better off living in a hedge. Well, obviously Larry, no-one sensible would have interpreted that as anything other than a minor expression of brief frustration. Clearly I didn't *actually mean it!* So when I got up the next morning and Black Chunky Cat and Grubby White Cat were both sitting underneath our garden table I was very surprised, especially when Black Chunky Cat said, *well here we are, Ghost, ready for biscuits on tap and a nice beanbag, but not to worry, we've found you a really lovely hedge.*

Larry! Imagine! Well, of course I wasn't at all upset or discombobulated. I just remembered, right at that moment, coincidentally, that I hadn't sprayed on the toaster plug socket to mark my territory recently; so I went and did that, but unfortunately, because the Employees have had the Very Silly Oversensitive Fusebox installed, it fused half the plugs and lights again, and First Employee had to dry it out with a hairdryer so he could get the coffee machine to work. So of course, none of that was my fault, but it was all very unsatisfactory.

Anyway, luckily Esso had been reading the North Buxton Monochrome Cat Alliance Memorandum and Articles of Association, and they say, interestingly; that, if cats are revealed to be a different colour in bright sunlight it doesn't affect their Monochrome Nature, because there is so little bright sunlight in Buxton that it is 'not material'. So I un-expelled Esso, and he went out to tell Chunky Black and Grubby White to bugger off, and he's going to come to the next meeting and 'sort things out properly under Any Other Business'. So that is all fine and no-one needs to think about the whole silly situation any more and especially about any part I might supposedly have played only if you put on it the most negative interpretation possible!

Lastly, Larry, Second Employee has almost finished her Utterly Ridiculous Crochet Blanket. She says she has got two rounds, a few flowers, and some weaving in to do. Second Employee is very bad at getting round to things though, Larry, so it will probably take her until Christmas 2025. I mention the situation, however, because I really think Second Employee is an inspiration here. Who would have thought that a slightly useless Employee could have expended so much time and effort and managed to produce... something even more useless? It really is incredible. But Esso says we are going to bring Second Employee back into the fold and teach her some tricks, so I will let you know how this goes, Larry. In the meantime, I shall be keeping a firm eye on the Petunias, and making sure Chunky Black Cat doesn't try to move in again!

**June 2023**

Larry, this is Esso, Ambassador to the High Peak and Minister for Aesthetic Standards... Larry, you may have heard the rumours about what happened yesterday. I shall be issuing a formal statement within the next couple of days when Ghost has worked out how to put a decent spin on things. In the meantime if Second Employee contacts you, can you remind her how I'm her special precious velvety Esso and best friend and how sad she would be if I was ever moved to another Embassy where TEETH don't matter quite as much? Thank you Larry, and I know if we all work together we can get through this minor PR challenge and come out stronger!

**June 2023**

Larry and the Catinet. This is Ghost, Ambassador to the High Peak and Shadow Minister for Aesthetic Standards, with my UPDATE and REPORT. Larry: I am broaching a difficult subject with you early, because I am still hopeful that, if we take swift action we can head off something RIDICULOUS if necessary. But before I get to that, Esso has asked me to issue a formal statement to exonerate him from having bitten Second Employee's Father again. Well, Larry, I began writing a statement in my INIMITABLE DEATHLESS PROSE but I have stopped. Because what can anyone say? What use are Weasel Words? Second Employee saw him do it, we have all seen the puncture wound on Second Employee's Father's Hand, Second Employee's Mother has started calling Esso Killer Bennett, and First Employee says he has been inspired by Esso and is going to start going round biting people himself.

Larry, it is no good biting people first and being sorry after, so I have told Esso to own his Shadow Side and to go Feral without fear, conscience, or favour, and to start by biting Second Employee every time she picks up her crochet hook because at least then we might be spared HORRORS like the Thing I noticed earlier which is 'going to be a cushion'. But of course he has not done. As soon as someone shows him a legitimate use for his Vice he is not interested. Instead, he has been curling up pointlessly on Second Employee's lap and PURRING and NUZZLING. Larry, can you make sure Second Employee properly understands what a fierce, unpredictable, violent BEAST Esso is, so she does not waste time cuddling him when she should be stroking me. Thank you.

Now, Larry, this brings me to my Difficult Subject. A few weeks ago, the Employees took Second Employee's Parents on a walk round Buxton to look at local gardens which Silly People open to the public on a particular weekend in June, causing their cats much inconvenience; particularly Basil, who lives across the road from the bookshop and who had to sit under a bench flicking his tail irritably all afternoon listening to people saying 'what a beautiful cat but I'm not sure he's friendly'. I *personally* think that First Employee in particular only went because he enjoys NOSING round other people's property, and because he knew one of the women who was exhibiting her garden and wanted to see if her house was bigger than the Embassy. That is my opinion. Esso says, that is nonsense, Ghost, you are only cynical because that is what you would do in those circumstances: but of course I would not. I do not have every listing on Rightmove within a 10-mile radius mentally catalogued and assessed like First Employee does. I am not a walking Zoopla Estimate. My mind is on higher things. Anyway, Second Employee has decided that next year she would like to exhibit the Embassy garden and welcome Buxton Locals to come and eat cake and criticise her Alliums. She has asked me, Larry, not to specify her motivation on my UPDATE as this is not a private group, and after much stroking I have agreed: but, Larry, let me assure you that her motivation is not noble. It is as far from noble as it can possibly be, although, I do have some sympathy. I shall, of course, not disclose confidential things, but I shall tell you an unrelated anecdote. A few months ago, Stubby-tailed Black Cat said to me at one of the meetings of the North Buxton Monochrome Cat Alliance, you're not much of a climber, are you, Ghost. Since then I have spent every night asleep on top of the suitcase on the wardrobe, and I have made sure Stubby-Tailed Black Cat knows it. You may draw your own conclusions. Anyway, I would like the advice of the Catinet: would it be possible for Second Employee, with concerted effort (ha!), to make the Embassy Garden interesting enough to welcome Nosy Locals next June? Cake will be provided. I am confident about the quality of the cake at least because Second Employee has certainly had enough practice, but for the rest I throw it open to the Catinet. You will notice Second Employee has not provided a photograph of the garden in its current state, and I would suggest there is a reason for that, but I have promised Esso I will not be negative about Second Employee's Passive-Aggressive Gardening. Anyway, Larry, I shall go, as Second Employee is muttering things about ordering Garden Arches, and I must go and stare at her intensely before any action is taken which cannot be recalled. I hope you are impressed, Larry, with how I am dealing with a Bitey Esso and Silly Employees - shall we have a Zoom at some point to discuss my transfer to Derbyshire Dales?

[Note from Ghost: we are currently 'rewilding the garden', and frankly I think that says everything there is to say about Second Employee's Gardening Competency. More effort needed methinks!]

## July 2023

Larry and the Catinet... Larry, this is Ghost from the High Peak, quickly dropping by to Deny Utterly the rumour that I have been

WITNESSED sitting on Second Employee's Ridiculous Crochet. It is Entirely Untrue. I am shunning it! Sometimes, Larry, one may wish to rest very briefly after the hard but important work of Cake Book Disapproval, and one may not be too discerning as to where one rests. That is all I will concede. As you know, Esso is the one who is In Thrall To Yarn. I just want to make that very, very clear before anyone suggests anything unhelpful. Thank you, Larry, and I shall do a proper update regarding the terrible Buxton weather and Second Employee's even worse hosting skills as soon as I have a moment. Could I also notify you for the record that I am still in discussions with the Goat Militia, just in case they might be useful in the future. They really are rather usefully Bellicose. I only mention this because Esso said the other day, Ghost, I do not want you whipping up Goat Militias on Zoom and promising them Skirmishes without mentioning it to anybody. So I have mentioned it. There is no need to be concerned.

Also, Larry, as an addendum to my Remarks about Names recently, I wish to notify you that Second Employee picked me up, showed me myself in the hallway mirror as if I wasn't already completely clear about what a very beautiful cat I am, and said the words, come on then, Mrs Slinky Malinki. Larry, could I ask you to check what or who is a Slinky Malinki and if this is something appropriate to be associated with Ambassadors?

## July 2023

Larry and the Catinet. This is Ghost, Ambassador to the High Peak and Shadow Minister for Aesthetic Standards, with my UPDATE. As a very, very special dispensation, Esso and I have recently allowed the Employees to have some of their 'friends' to stay at the Embassy. Well, firstly, Larry, I don't see why Employees need 'friends'. I personally think it encourages them in Silliness and stops them paying proper attention to their work. Anyway, I do not think it works having 'friends' coming to stay, because Buxton only really works for Very Brave Ambassadors who are Adventurous and Robust About Weather.

Firstly, Larry, although our first visitors did not come from far away, they managed to take four and a half hours to drive here because it was 'quite confusing after you come off the M1 and there was heavy rain on the Ashbourne road'. Well, Larry, the Ashbourne road is always challenging. First Employee says the fog is often so bad in winter he cannot see where he is going at all. So I would firstly like to recommend that all 'friends' go on an Introduction To Buxton course before their visit where they are introduced to techniques for driving with zero visibility, dealing with rain the 'like of which they have never actually seen in England before', and having an opinion on the current controversy, the Geese in Pavilion Gardens: Are They Too Troublesome, Or Not.

[Note from Esso: Ghost occasionally tries to organise the Pavilion Gardens Geese for her own ends but it is unsuccessful because they really are terribly troublesome and far too anarchic to fit into the Strategic Plan.]

So then, Larry, flushed with our Hosting Success, we had another 'friend', who had an interest in Archaeology and made the Employees go looking at Stone Circles and climbing up rocks in the rain. I personally think this is setting a very bad example, particularly for Second Employee, who tells everyone she is a Pagan if she is given any encouragement at all and is prone to wandering off being unhelpful and talking about Strong Energies and other such nonsense. In fact I am always concerned she may start doing something Widdershins while Skyclad in the back garden which would be very alarming for Graham next door and the drug dealer down the road!

Anyway, I particularly disapproved of this Archaeology Friend, because he was some kind of AI Academic, and told us all we had evolved beyond the need for human interaction and would be taken over entirely by AI probably before the end of next week. Obviously, Larry, that would be annoying and inconvenient and would have terrible implications for the Strategic Plan. Esso says it is good for us to be challenged by new ideas and we must not become too provincial, and that he himself thought it was all *terribly* interesting, although he will of course still need Second Employee to love him and stroke him after we have replaced human interaction with chat bots: but Second Employee told the 'friend' to 'bugger off back to the City and take your Apocalypse with you', which was Inappropriately Rude, although understandable. Esso says she was just joking: but Larry, as you know, Second Employee is a particularly humourless Employee, so I imagine this is unlikely.

And besides, she has subsequently said that next time she will 'sit him in a room with Interim Summer Employee and they can have an argument about the Turing Test and I shall go to Meadowhall'. Larry, can you pass a law stopping Second Employee from going to Meadowhall when we have particularly challenging Visitors who she needs to Deal With. Thank you.

Also, Larry, a couple of other things. The Employees wandered back home yesterday with Two Enormous Gold creatures, lined them up in front of the fireplace, and Second Employee announced they were 'part of her Foo Dog collection'. Well, Larry, that is fine, because I shall also have a collection, and it will be of Competent Employees Who Are Not Second Employee And Do Not Collect Silly Things, and I shall probably start collecting next week via a recruitment advert in How To Be A Good Employee Magazine.

And one last thing: can I let all members of the Catinet know to AVOID Sheffield for a month from this coming Thursday at all costs. Second Employee's Silly Artist Brother is having a Silly

Art Exhibition, and if people go to it it might encourage him, and he might produce more paintings of Sausage Rolls. And if that happens I shall be Exceptionally Cross. As you can see, Larry, there has been a lot going on here of which I have had to Strongly Disapprove: and in between Disapproving of Silly Visitors, Gilded Foo Dogs, and Potential Hyperrealist Renditions in Oil of Greggs Sausage Rolls, I really am almost exhausted!

**July 2023**

Larry and the Catinet. This is Esso, Ambassador to the High Peak and Minister for Aesthetic Standards with an extensive Report on Art Appreciation. Larry, I would be terribly grateful if you could avoid mentioning it to Ghost: but I gave the Employee's permission to go to Second Employee's Brother's First Art Exhibition, because I really think it's important for Employees to cultivate an appreciation of Art, even if it's Art featuring something Ghost doesn't approve of, like sausage rolls. Well, Larry, the Employees had a great time: but something happened which I'm afraid we must keep from Ghost forever. Second Employee's Brother And Partner had planned the exhibition very carefully, and it was in a PUB in Sheffield: and they had put together Goody Bags which featured Fun Things like Lighters and Beermats which had been signed by Second Employee's Brother: and Second Employee's Brother's Partner went round and gave everyone a Gregg's Sausage Roll in a bag, with a choice of either Meat or

Vegan. This was the catering. Second Employee says it was Witty and Ironic and she enjoyed her vegan sausage roll very much.

Although Second Employee is not Vegan, she says she used to buy Vegan Sausage Rolls from a shop when she lived in Cambridge, and she enjoyed them, too. She told me that once she had a chest infection and Laryngitis, which is a DISEASE Employees occasionally get where they can't speak, and in fact it might be a blessing to all of us perhaps if First Employee would get it once in a while, but he is very robust. Anyway, she said she felt iller than she has ever felt in her life, and literally actually thought she would die from the coughing because she is an Asthmatic Employee and sometimes a little feeble in terms of lungs. So she said as she lay coughing on the sofa one night gasping for breath, she thought about how her partner who she lived with then would leave her to die rather than helping her get to Casualty because he would have thought he was too important to lose the sleep. And in fact, that was why she had to be on the sofa to start with, so he was not disturbed, because he considered himself to be quite a significant bit more important than she was, because he was an Intellectual.

[Note from Esso. It is fair to say that Second Employee is not an Intellectual. And she does not have to be! She is clever enough to stroke me and to put the biscuits in the dish! Any more

CLEVERNESS than that in Employees is CLEVERNESS wasted!]

So she said she spent the time when she was lying on the sofa, coughing and gasping and not having *absolutely the best time* she had ever had, thinking of all the people she knew who her then partner did not like her talking to but who would have helped her to not die if she had rung them. And she said her brother was one of the people at the top of the list. So those were her thoughts on that quite long night of no breathing.

Can you imagine that, Larry. I personally love people to stroke me and disturb me when I am asleep. I PURR and stretch out and NUZZLE them, and if the Employees are ever ill in the night Ghost and I make sure to keep them company. In fact, the night Second Employee had Norovirus, Ghost kept so close that Second Employee almost had to vault over her to get to the toilet and still talks about it to this day. So she must have felt very supported. And in fact that is very good for Employees with Norovirus, as you know: keeping them moving and even jumping up and down a bit. It was so effective that we added it to the Strategic Plan!

Anyway, of course it turned out that Second Employee didn't die. She got up in the morning, and was better enough to ring the doctor finally and make herself understood by shouting at the absolute top of her voice, which the receptionist heard as a whisper: because of course her partner had been too busy and important to be able to ring for her before. And then finally the doctor could give her antibiotics, and then her *very first action* on being able to walk into town again was to go to the Vegan Sausage Roll shop and mime 'I would like a Vegan Sausage Roll Please' to the man behind the counter.

I dread to think, Larry, what that mime involved, because Second Employee is not an Employee who is very good at physical expression at the best of times and there are so many ways it could have been Inappropriate. But Second Employee got her sausage roll all those years ago, and recovered. And the Employees had an excellent time at the exhibition and got another sausage roll, and Second Employee says sometimes she looks back and sees LINKS and considers them to be a 'curious synchronicity'. So Second Employee's Brother's Art is now formally launched upon the world, and we will keep it secret from Ghost because she only needs to know about modern art on a need-to-know basis and she really is quite busy at the moment keeping an eye on Graham next door!

**July 2023**

Larry, this is Ghost, Ambassador to the High Peak. Larry, the Employees are looking SHIFTY and I am concerned about what they might be planning. When I walk into rooms looking FABULOUS with my tail PROUDLY ALOFT, I sometimes catch them whispering together, saying things like, how long are we going to be on the ferry, have you got your acupressure bands, how hot is it going to be. Larry, I want to say this to you formally and I would like it to be properly recorded: if the Employees are considering going abroad again, I am washing my hands of them. I have had these discussions with Esso. I know he thinks, Larry, that if we allow them to leave the country it will be good for them and teach them resilience and all sorts of NONSENSE THINGS, but you and I know this is not true, and that Esso's naivety is now so extreme I actually *personally* consider it to be almost criminal.

If the Employees leave the country this year things will go badly. I have seen it written in the patterns of the leaves and the flight of the swifts and the calls of the jackdaws and also I just know that it is what will happen because they are REALLY USELESS.

Can we have this properly recorded that I have said it, Larry, and if they go trotting off with their lightweight linen and their sun cream and their insect repellent then I am not having them back when they have messed things up. Thank you. And I shall not hold back in saying I Told You So. I mean I do not hold back anyway, but I shall doubly not hold back. In fact, I will follow Esso around and wherever he is I will pop up and say it. There he will be, eating his biscuits for example. Esso! I told you so!

Lying on the spare room bed. Esso! You were a naive fool! Yes, Larry, I shall make everyone in this household Rue The Day!

**August 2023**

Larry, this is Ghost, Ambassador to the High Peak. I'm very annoyed to have to AGAIN refute allegations that I've been seen KNEADING on Second Employee's Silly Crochet Blanket. Can I assure you that I am NOT, and NEVER HAVE BEEN, a secret crochet lover, whatever rumours may or may not be flying about on WhatsApp groups. It is absolutely untrue to say that I find crochet 'comforting' and that I 'enjoy the feeling of double front post trebles under my toe beans', and I am really very, very cross. I shall track down the source of these allegations, Larry, and when I do, even the Strategic Plan won't save them!

**August 2023**

Larry and the Catinet. This is Esso, Ambassador to the High Peak, and Minister for Aesthetic Standards. Larry, I have made a decision, rightly or wrongly, and I am notifying you of it just in case anyone theoretically might ever need support extracting Employees from difficulties in the Bay of Biscay, or from any minor disagreements with the Guardia Civil, for example. I am sending the Employees to Spain And Portugal for three weeks in line with the Continued Employee Professional Development

Strategy 23-24. Second Employee doesn't want to go, but it will do her good: frankly, in recent weeks she has started suggesting that she thinks Whaley Bridge is 'a long way away and exotic', which is not healthy, Larry. I think we all need to try to remember that there's a whole other world out there. As you know, Ghost and I once made the incredibly intrepid journey to Buxton from Chesterfield Cats' Protection: frankly, I believe a journey like that is almost unparalleled. We can't, obviously, expect the Employees to be quite as adventurous, but I do feel we stand as a fine example of the values of Travel, Exploration, and Adapting To New Cultures!

Ghost says it's a ridiculous thing to do and the Employees should stay here and everyone knows her views and they are Very Much Anti. I have told her that it will give them useful new ideas to make them more effective in their work: but she says that we all know that the last time Second Employee went to Spain the only ideas she came back with were a/ that Spanish hotels serve doughnuts for breakfast, and b/ that the next time she went she should take her own teabags, because apparently she once asked for a cup of tea with her breakfast up a mountain in Donostia and was given a Liptons Green Tea Teabag and a small pyrex cup of hot, not boiling, water.

It is true, I am afraid, that we have not heard the end of it since. Ghost says Second Employee is the 'worst kind of Little Englander' and we should leave her to it with her 'ridiculous scones and her ridiculous Homemade Plum Jam and her ridiculous Emma Bridgewater mugs she buys at the end of the sale for 70% off because who wants a Beaver on a mug, Esso, they can't give them away', but Larry, I think Second Employee can still be redeemed! Besides, it's time for Interim Summer Employee to start his next Martial Arts Training Programme with me, before he forgets everything he's learned! I really feel if I have a good go at him for three weeks - and if we can avoid the entirely accidental 'opening a vein with a claw' which really only ever happened once - I might be able to get him at least to Advanced Beginner.

So Larry, if you could just keep an eye on things via your International Contacts for the next 3 weeks, that would be great. Ghost has said to me, Esso, if those Employees come back with anything other than a New Found Addiction To Portuguese Custard Tarts I shall not be responsible for my actions... but I, Esso, Minister for Aesthetic Standards, am sure it will be fine! I shall do my Duty here with Interim Summer Employee, the Employees will do their duty right down from Madrid to the Costa Del Sol, and I shall have no concerns at all!

**August 2023**

Larry, and the Catinet. This is Ghost, Ambassador to the High Peak and Shadow Minister for Aesthetic Standards to tell you what a very SILLY and RIDICULOUS thing Esso has done!

Larry, I told you this would happen. He gave the Employees permission to go GALLIVANTING round SPAIN and PORTUGAL and all sorts of ridiculous places for three weeks - I knew they were planning something! - and he didn't tell me until it was too late! He said, I knew you would have caused trouble, Ghost, but it's good for them. Good for them!

Well, I would, and I would have been right to do it, because the Employees, as I predicted, have got into all sorts of trouble. I have managed to make WhatsApp contact with Second Employee, and all I can say is, I am banning her from ever going away again. Larry, she is not capable. Esso's confidence was utterly misplaced. Firstly, they have caused trouble in Portugal by continually wanting milk in coffee, but not as much as they were given: and then they drove through the border checkpoint and the wrong toll lanes at 100 miles an hour and 'didn't realise they should have stopped'. Second Employee said she 'had the vague idea until we got to Spain that the car had automatically converted to show kmph rather than mph which was obviously very silly, but now she realises she will make First Employee go slower' - this will show you, Larry, the level of intellect we are dealing with.

And as a final insult, Larry, Second Employee managed to slip *for no visible reason* right in the middle of the Praça do Comércio in Lisbon, fall on her arm, and break it: and now she is a USELESS EMPLOYEE for twenty eight days until she gets her cast off. Larry, I am furious, and I can *absolutely guarantee you* that she'll still manage to pick up some ridiculous things for the house even with one arm in a sling and even though she can't fasten her own bra.

Esso says this is all fine because it is teaching the Employees resourcefulness, co-operation, and resilience, and besides we are fine here with Interim Summer Employee who is competent; but Larry that is all nonsense apart from the bit about Interim Summer Employee which I concede is true. I am furious. I am about to begin an extensive Zoom with my Andalucian Goat Militia, but could you also please contact the Border Police, the Guardia Civil, Britannia Ferries and the competent woman on the till at the Comares Coviran and for God's sake get them to organise the Employees and bring them back to England before they ruin my reputation any more than they have done already!

**August 2023**

Larry, this is Ghost again. Larry, I have been in contact with Second Employee again, and she is feeling very sorry for herself. She says her cast is very hot, and Spain is very hot, and the Spanish House which belongs to First Employee from when he was living his life of shallow hedonism in Spain previous to marrying her is very hot: and mostly she herself is very hot. So all in all she is not managing terribly well, as predicted by me. I have no sympathy. She says when she went to the doctor on the Costa Del Sol to have her wrist looked at, he took one look at her in her pale pink linen looking a little washed out and said, look at the colour of you: *what are you even doing here*? And Second Employee was slightly taken aback. And then began to ask herself the same question.

And then the doctor made it far worse, because he turned Second Employee's arms over to look at the underside, which was very pale: and said, oh my *God,* look at you, you must not leave the house, you must stay out of the sun and you must only go out before 9am and after 7pm otherwise you will *burn right up*. I mean, Larry, that is Second Employee's fault for wafting about in pale pink linen looking feeble, I have told her before that her penchant for Gudrun Sjöden doesn't benefit anyone; and in fact whoever Gudrun Sjöden is she would do much better designing things with a more structured fabric and a tailored waist; that is my opinion.

Anyway, Second Employee says they then brought on another man, who was presumably also a doctor although one never knows with Second Employee, in fact for all she ever checks he may have been the man who had come to deliver an Evri parcel or check the water meter: anyway, he quickly wrapped her arm up in wet plaster whoosh whoosh whoosh just like that. And by the time she realised it was going to be a big heavy plaster cast it was set and it was too late: and when she said she couldn't cope with a big heavy cast the man said his English wasn't good enough to listen to protests of that nature, and she would just have to put up with the situation, and that was that.

So Second Employee says she is going to learn Spanish properly on Duolingo so that no-one can ever sneak a cast on her again without her explicit consent, and in the meantime she is sitting with a fan trained on her and eating Nectarines and Principe Galletas con Crema de Chocolate and trying to find enough 4G to WhatsApp people and moan: and I really think that in the future what we need to do is Chip the Employees or perhaps fit collars so that they get a small electric shock any time they try to leave Derbyshire.

Esso says this is a really terrible thing to say or even to think, and it is very important for Employees to have free will and autonomy and I have really got to think about my Controlling Nature. Well, Esso is talking nonsense! I only said a small electric shock! I'm not even advocating for anything fatal!

Not at this stage.

Second Employee said, could you just have a look at Duolingo, Ghost, and see how it works because you're so clever and I''m so hot and blah blah blah. Well, I had a look, and it seems to be a lot of NONSENSE about guilting people with an Owl: and who needs that kind of thing. I can guilt people myself, without an owl needing to be involved at all. And it teaches you to say quite pointless things, for example, the pigs live on the farm, or, last night I met Juan and we danced the tango. None of these are useful things for Second Employee to learn: what she needs to be able to say, is, *I have been very silly, and I need to find my way back to my employment in the High Peak in England without causing anyone any further trouble, can you get me on to the next ferry please*. I think when she finally makes it back I shall teach both of the Employees to say that very phrase in at least all of the major European languages and possibly Tagalog as well!

# Chapter 5
# Autumn 2023: Home Improvements

**September 2023**

Larry and the Catinet; this is Esso, Ambassador to the High Peak, and Minister for Aesthetic Standards. Oh dear, Larry. Oh dear. The Employees are back, after driving 2,333 miles through Spain and Portugal. I was hoping it would make them better, more cultured, more resilient Employees: but Ghost says they're exactly the same Employees they were before, just a bit fatter from all that time sitting in the car arguing about what album to listen to, and from eating Almond Cake for breakfast every day.

They seem to have become increasingly focused, Larry, on procuring the right kind of tea and coffee on their travels, to the extent that Second Employee even appears to have travelled with her own teabags, which she does at least have the grace to be ashamed of. Luckily, Ghost hasn't questioned the large objects wrapped in bubble wrap which have appeared on the dining room table yet: I had to give Second Employee permission while she was away to 'buy a few tiny bits for the house to make her feel better', but they've come back with two enormous Moroccan lanterns which they're going to hang above the dining table. Well, I'm not sure there's even room for them to start with, because they really are rather large: but Second Employee said, look Esso, I had a broken arm, heat exhaustion, and a stomach bug: I had to make a quick decision, and I always think with dining room light fittings, go big or go home.

Well, Larry. Well. Oh dear. I'm fairly sure Ghost doesn't always think go big or go home with dining room light fittings, whatever the physical pressures: and all I can hope is that the Employees have run out of money (again) for an electrician to fit them until at least next year, when I might have worked out a way to Finesse Things.

Also, Larry, I quizzed First Employee very, very firmly about whether he made sure he always drove to the speed limit and paid all the appropriate road tolls, especially in Portugal, where apparently 'it was often quite unclear': and, frankly, I found him disingenuous and obfuscatory. I do not think that is too strong a description. Indeed, at one point he said to me, Esso, what happens in Portugal stays in Portugal. Larry, this suggests to me that there may be some minor irregularities: would it be possible just to have a quick look and see if First Employee is featuring prominently on any kind of International Database Of Traffic Criminals? And if Interpol might perhaps need paying off, or bribing? Many thanks.

Also, Larry, Second Employee came home with the most enormous plaster cast on her arm, apparently from falling over in Lisbon. Ghost said we must just ignore it, because she was clearly only doing it for attention and to get through passport control quicker: and luckily she has been to Buxton Hospital today where a very firm nurse said to her, whatever they might or might not do on the Costa Del Sol where Second Employee had seen a doctor, in Buxton we do not have people wandering around looking like that. It is inappropriate. So now Second Employee has a removable splint, and is much happier. I mean, I think she might well be back up to full speed even by October. Ghost says it's too late, she's going to terminate her contract and have Interim Summer Employee as Permanent Employee, because whatever one might say about him he's at least managed never to just fall over randomly and break something. But Larry, Second Employee and I are Best Friends and I would like to keep her, please, if possible, even at a slightly reduced service.

It is a little bit of a reduced service at the moment, too, because she's still dizzy from the boat. Earlier I allowed her out to take her overdue books back to the library and she nearly fell over in Oxfam and took out three Buxton locals, a display of lettuce seeds and a pottery cat. I'm not even sure what she was doing in Oxfam, so I've had to restrict her movements further, and at the moment I'm only allowing her out with pre-approval of her itinerary, which seems to be working well.

Larry, I have a question for the Catinet: do other Employees react badly to ferry crossings? Ghost says it doesn't surprise her that Second Employee cannot cope, because she is unspeakably feeble, and in fact it hasn't affected First Employee at all; so she is probably putting it on. But I have googled, and it can be very choppy in the Bay of Biscay: and the Employees were on the boat for twenty four hours, so it may indeed have been difficult! I would just like to prove to Ghost that Second Employee is no more feeble than other Employees, Larry, so I can keep her without an argument: and hopefully Ghost also won't find out about the Moroccan lanterns, or notice her looking for recipes for Spanish Almond Cake and Portuguese Custard Tarts.

It's not easy to deal with Ambassador/ Employee relations: but at least the weather is nice (and not forty eight degrees like the Employees said it was in Seville), there are no new silly blue tables, and we are all together again!

[Note from Esso: the Catinet were very helpful here, and reassured me that their own Employees also sometimes have trouble with BOATS, and that Second Employee is not unusual in this respect. I was listening our own Employees chatting the other day, and First Employee was saying, *Susie, you cannot cope with boats, you're frightened of flying, and you don't like long car journeys; what do you think our best option is here.* And Second Employee said, *our best option is not leaving the house at all but staying on the sofa and drinking our own nice coffee which is delicious.* I think this may be indicative of something Ghost has pointed out before, i.e. that the best solution for people who don't like BOATS is, above all, not to marry other people who do like BOATS. Ghost says the whole pairing up in Employees thing is so ridiculously random that she thinks we should change the system and allocate matches based on what people's Feline Employers know of their character. Although I entirely see Ghost's point and in fact I think she is right, I really don't want to go down this route at the moment because it would be an enormous amount of work. I may, however, agree to add it to a future Strategic Plan.]

## September 2023

Larry and the Catinet. This is Ghost, Ambassador to the High Peak and Proper Minister For Aesthetic Standards Who Is Better Than Esso. Larry, I have promoted myself and I am booting Esso out of his Ministership, because frankly since he strode in through the catflap that day and declared he was now Aesthetic Standards Minister things have got even worse around here. Not only that but I have decided I am Head Of The Pressure Group For Banning Handicrafts; there is no-one else in it at the moment, but give me a fortnight and we will be a force to be reckoned with. So could you just notify Esso formally of all these things so he isn't difficult. Thank you.

Now, Larry, just as Second Employee's Broken Wrist was getting a tiny bit better and we had celebrated a number of milestones such as her being able to spray her own deodorant and fasten her bra without input from First Employee, she managed to develop a Family Crisis and an Ear Infection at the same time, which she did on purpose; because not one single sensible part of the Strategic Plan, frankly, has been delivered all week. Instead she has been SITTING ABOUT lazily visiting people in Acute Frailty Units and Fretting Pointlessly about stairlifts and falls and *nonsense*, and then coming home and sitting on the sofa looking stunned, which meets no KPI that I know of! Esso says she is now on antibiotics and will be better soon, but that is too long for me - besides, who knows about the Family Crisis?!

And moreover, Larry, while I was PATROLLING the chest of drawers in the Employee Bedroom earlier to make sure Second Employee is not being LAZY and is putting her laundry away in a timely fashion (she is not), I found an item. It is very difficult to describe adequately: it seems to be a Small Ceramic Red Devil, particularly incompetently executed. Indeed I WhatsApped a picture of it to the Team surrounding the Dark Force and they agreed with me that it really looked nothing like him and in fact he was quite offended, but Larry I have never been a CAT who has worried about offending the Dark Force in the past, so I am certainly not going to start now!

I think, frankly, that the presence of this Silly Item says *everything* about the impossibility of ever making the Employees Aesthetically Acceptable. It was *clearly* purchased on their travels abroad, despite everything I said to them. Esso said, oh Ghost actually that has always been there, you have just not noticed it before; so, Larry, perhaps you could clarify with Esso that I was not, in fact, born yesterday, and that if he tells Shocking Fibs then he will not go to Cat Heaven to be with Bast at the end of his nine lives, whereas I, am who am always truthful, will, and I will get his share of Heavenly Biscuits.

And what is more, everybody thinks I *do not know* about the Moroccan Lanterns, and did not hear James The Electrician in *our very kitchen* the other day saying, well, possibly it might work if I screw them into a ceiling plate and hang them from a brass chain: but, as I have said previously, I hear things, and I see things, and I know things: and, Larry, you and I both know this does not portend anything good, and James should have more sense! And also, James perhaps ought to remember that I know where his mother lives, and I know what her weaknesses are.

Anyway. You will be pleased to learn that I have taken proper action. I am replacing Second Employee, and I have put an advert to that effect in How To Be A Better Employee Magazine:

Wanted: Employee for busy, professional Embassy. Must be physically robust, possibly without ears, and preferably with no family who are likely to sit around in the Embassy for hours and say, hasn't your cat got unusual markings, has she put on weight round her bottom. Must commit to never being related to the type of artists who are likely to give her/ him large inappropriate paintings, especially of sausage rolls. All candidates must understand profound importance of Employers peeing on toaster plug when required and must be appropriately appreciative, despite any very minor inconvenience caused. Experience of Strategic Plan delivery a must. Desirable: should smell exactly the same as current Employee and should be willing to sit for long periods stroking whiskers back from Employer cheeks and allowing Employer to KNEAD on head, with claws. Should also understand that TEETH occasionally act independently, and should not be SILLY about it. Also: equal commitment both to making Embassy a machine for living à la Le Corbusier, and stroking Employers while saying, Ghostycat you are the prettiest and softest cat in the ENTIRETY of the High Peak. Both to be tested by presentation/ practical at interview. Applications via CV with covering letter to very_soft_ghostycat@highpeakembassy.gov.uk.

We will not tell Esso just yet, Larry: I will see what applications I get and go from there. It has been a hard road: but I really think, thanks to me, that this may be the start of a new and efficient way forward!

## September 2023

Larry and the Catinet, this is Esso, Ambassador to the High Peak and Minister for Aesthetic Standards, *whatever Ghost says*, with my update. Larry, I find myself in the thick of a MYSTERY. I could ask Ghost what she was doing, but you know what Ghost is like: so I thought I'd ask you first if you knew anything about it.

I heard her on a Zoom call the other day as I walked past Second Employee's 'office' AKA the room with the sewing machine and the quilting mat in it. She was saying, well, thanks for this because I just thought we could have a little chat over Zoom before I convene the interview panel and everyone else has OPINIONS. Well, Larry, I wondered what was going on: so I LURKED outside the door, and I heard another, rather firm, voice say, that's no problem at all, Ghost. Thank you for sending me the photographs of the Embassy, and I can reassure you that by the time I've been in post a week I'll have 95% of all of that nonsense in the Recycling Centre and the rest will be ashes in a fire pit on the patio.

As you can imagine: this *piqued* my interest. So I listened for Ghost's reply, although she was a little slower than I expected: but then she said, well, of course that's all excellent, but I do think we should just check first if anything's worth any money; for example the Employees did get those giant Foo Dogs from an Antiques Fair... and then the other, firm voice interrupted, and said, Ghost, come now; you and I both know that whoever sold those Foo Dogs to Second Employee probably bought them at the Range for £2.99 the day before or possibly the clearance shelf at Chesterfield TK Maxx for £4.95 and that's the most generous interpretation I can possibly put on things.

Then I heard Ghost say, well yes of course, and obviously it will be good to start off with a clean slate for efficient Strategic Plan delivery... but I did notice that one thing you didn't address on your CV was how you intend to let me know I'm the softest cat in the High Peak and how you would go about things re Stroking. Larry, I confess I listened again: and this time, the firm voice said, I'm afraid I won't be getting involved in that kind of thing: and besides, frankly, it's statistically unlikely, isn't it, whatever nonsense Second Employee has told you? I think the best I can do is to say I might pat you on the head occasionally and tell you you're softer than Esso, although I *will* have to verify that; because I'll warn you I've seen a photo of him and he looks extremely velvety: but I'm entirely confident that my proven track record in Strategic Plan Delivery will compensate for any other silly things you might think you want!

Well, Larry, I tried to peep into the room at that point to see who was on the screen: but Ghost started to look round, so I ran away swiftly and silently until I had gone down three flights of stairs and I was safe on the piano stool, with all my LEGGIES in the air. I think I caught a glimpse of a rather severe hairstyle, and some charcoal linen: but I'm not sure.

Can you solve the mystery, Larry? I wondered if perhaps Ghost was interviewing someone for her column in How To Be A Good Employee Magazine: but who knows! She hasn't said anything about it, but I have noticed her following Second Employee round and CHIRRUPING and TRILLING, and rolling over to put her Fluffy Underneath on display: and every time, Second Employee strokes her and says, Ghost, you are so soft and beautiful and precious, you are the softest cat not only in the High Peak but also in Tameside and the whole of Greater Manchester. And Ghost purrs!

Also, Larry, can I just reassure you that any rumours you might have heard that I bit Second Employee right on her broken wrist are, of course, completely untrue: but, if they did by any (malicious) interpretation of the (disputed) facts have any veracity at all, I'd like to point out that Second Employee herself said the following; well he might as well bite me there because I've got a splint on and I can't feel it; which led First Employee to remark that 'possibly the best way to deal with Esso was for everyone to wear armour'. So all is entirely well, Larry, and we are all ready, able and enthusiastic for a full, productive week of Delivering The Strategic Plan!

**September 2023**

Larry, this is Ghost, Ambassador to the High Peak and Minister For Aesthetic Standards No Matter What Esso Says, and Larry, Second Employee has PROPPED a silly picture in my Special Skulking Place, which states in large text on a pink background 'ART IS WHAT YOU CAN GET AWAY WITH'! Is she mocking me, Larry? Because if she is mocking me I shall restart my recruitment procedure, I shall push it through to a conclusion, and I shall Not Waver. However, for the moment I have made the decision to put things on ice and just see how things go. I *did* have a suitable applicant, but there were just a couple of the essential criteria I *very slightly* queried her commitment to delivering, although she really did do fabulously well in the charcoal linen department.

While we're on the subject, Larry, I wonder if you know anyone who could just check if those Foo Dogs are worth anything, or if they are just probably from the clearance shelf at TK Maxx - which some people (who apparently think it's beneath them to stroke Ambassadors even though they really are extremely soft which is constantly verified by Second Employee despite all her faults) - might think? Thank you, Larry. I was just interested.

**October 2023**

Larry and the Catinet. This is Ghost, Ambassador to the High Peak and the REAL Minister for Aesthetic Standards Whatever Esso Says.

Larry, a couple of things I need to keep you updated on. Firstly, I was looking in the Strategic Plan for Second Employee's Job Description just in case theoretically I might ever want to start the capability procedure, and I found a handwritten piece of paper stapled to the back. It said 'Second Employee Job Role Essential Skills: 1/ Eating Cake 2/ Wearing Dungarees Despite Criticism. All Second Employees should only EVER be assessed against these two criteria'.

Well, Larry, you and I both know this was never in the original Strategic Plan, whatever Esso says! He's clearly added it later! It was handwritten and stapled in! Anyway, I confronted him, and he gave me some nonsense about it having been adopted at the last Strategic Plan Review, which it was not: and told me it could only be removed by 'a quorum'. So I said, well, Esso, what are you pretending constitutes a Quorum, and he said, me and Veronica, which, Larry, cannot be true.

In fact, Larry, I may not have introduced Veronica. She is lodging with us temporarily: she says she isn't keen on the cold, so she's waiting for a nice day and then she's going to make use of it to set off for Dove Holes. I don't know why, Larry, we seem to be forever providing Temporary Accommodation for the larger species of Arachnid, but that does seem to be the case, and I hold my tongue for the moment. Esso says they often bring interesting new ideas to the table, and that may be true, but making them part of Quora is something else; and I am sure there is something in the Memorandum and Articles of Association of the Embassy which I can use to prove to Esso he is talking Utter Nonsense. It's just that I *do not really want* to have to read them to find out.

And anyway, I will never be able to persuade Veronica to do anything sensible or helpful, because the last time she came out for an evening constitutional Second Employee saw her, SCREAMED, and shouted Jesus Christ, look at the size of that Effing Spider. It was all I could do to stop Veronica putting in a formal grievance, because she said not only had she been Fat Shamed but she was also a committed Christian and objected to Second Employee's language. It was only when I told her that I PERSONALLY had seen her recharging her energy by being Skyclad in the Full Moon on the garden table, and that that wasn't the action of any committed Christian that I knew of, that she agreed to rethink!

So Larry, it is all very difficult, but could you tell Esso to stop making up NONSENSE and un-staple the SILLY BIT OF PAPER so I can start the capability procedure properly. Thank you.

Also, Second Employee has had a Birthday. Esso bought her a Silly Book, and said, look, Ghost, that will make everything clearer to her and stop all your little niggles. Well, all I will say about that is that if a year's worth of Intelligent and Well-Directed Opinion Pieces by Yours Truly in How To Be A Better Employee Magazine have not made one iota of difference then I fail to see a book called How To Communicate With Your Cat will.

And finally, there is a Huge Danger that I need to flag up. The Employees have decided to put a New Kitchen in the Embassy even though it is a waste of money which could be spent on Cat Food or on becoming better Employees. I have looked carefully through their New Kitchen Brochures, and I think I can confidently say that it appears to be illegal to buy a kitchen which isn't grey, so I am reasonably confident they can't mess it up: but there is always the risk. I have therefore chosen the kitchen which I, personally, think is appropriate. Esso said, Ghost, that will not work, you know the Employees are not bright enough to deal with kitchen doors which don't have handles on. Indeed, Second Employee's Mother has a Cream Shiny Handleless Kitchen, and whenever the Employees go there, they spend their entire time pushing impotently and sadly at doors in an utterly random fashion, waiting for one to spring open and reveal the teabags: and then when it finally happens the teabags turn out to be decaf, which is disappointing, although Second Employee's Brother is now leading the fightback and has managed to introduce a small packet of Caffeinated Strong Assam.

Well, whatever Esso says about Employee Inadequacy, I have decided we must put Aesthetics over Function, so Larry, if it is not actually illegal to have a kitchen which is not grey, could you make it so quickly before the Employees manage to do anything SILLY. Thank you. As you can see, Larry, it all continues to be quite exhausting; but at least I manage to snatch a few restful moments when I can!

**October 2023**

Larry - just a quick one - it's me, Esso, Ambassador to the High Peak and Minister for Aesthetic Standards In Difficult Circumstances. I'm afraid I know something about the new Embassy Kitchen that might possibly make Ghost kick off just a tiny bit, so before I talk to her I just wondered if I could check re diplomatic immunity and all that jazz... Many thanks, Larry! I'll just have a little lie down in the meantime and gather my strength for what's to come!

## October 2023

Larry and the Catinet, it's me, Ghost, with an Accurate Observation.

Larry: I personally feel that in this world there are a number of Unhelpful Things which lead Employees into Folly and Inappropriateness. Some of those things in particular have glossy covers and can either be purchased at unjustifiable expense in WH Smiths, or come through the door because First Employee gets them free with one of his bank accounts. And that is very much on First Employee. You are not telling me that he couldn't ask the bank to give him a subscription to something useful instead; for instance, to pluck an example out of thin air, How To Be A Better Employee Magazine. Or, perhaps, a magazine that is *vaguely* political so Second Employee could read it and become better informed and make tutting noises, but not so political that she is inspired to do anything involving a Placard.

Anyway, you get the idea: surely it is theoretically possible for Second Employee to be kept away from things like Pinterest or Instagram or Country Living Magazine where she keeps reading about women of a similar age to her who manage to conquer their natural desire to sit quietly with a cup of tea for long enough to Renovate Houses. It is not good for her. I do not want Second Employee being inspired by anybody sourcing silly handmade tiles in Morocco or Mexico or Ipswich or wherever these things come from. I do not want her to learn about Jemima from Hampshire who moved to a charmingly rural renovated dairy after her divorce, painted it fuchsia pink, gold leafed the toilet ceiling, and called the whole silly business 'dopamine decor'. I don't want her to learn about people who print their own wallpaper in a rustic shed POINTLESSLY with a hand-carved wooden block. I *particularly* don't want her to learn about people who breed their own sheep from which they knit their own jumpers and who have a lovely authentic spinning wheel in the sitting room along with a milking stool *quite arbitrarily*. All of these things are nonsense, and, worse, I think they *actively corrupt* Second Employee when what she really needs to do is to think about the wonderful aesthetic benefits of living somewhere that is sensibly grey and not putting anything in it that we do not need for me to sleep on; note, I said *me* and not *Esso*.

So, if you could restrict Second Employee's Social Media Viewing, Larry, only to Minimalist People and Uncontroversial News Stories, I think that would be for the best until this dangerous time of Kitchen Improvements has past.

In the meantime, can I just notify you that Esso is hanging about looking shifty: I'm going to assume there's no reason, but I'm just flagging it up as a danger; because the last time this happened it turned out that he had prior knowledge of a quite complicated Cabinet plot involving Matt Hancock and didn't really know what to do with the information!

## October 2023

Larry, this is Esso, Ambassador to the High Peak - Larry, Ghost came to me earlier and fixed me with a LOOK, and said, Esso, if there is something you need to get off your chest, Mister, now is the time to do it.

Larry, I couldn't tell her. The fact is, that despite her having decided on a Sensible Matt Grey Kitchen for the Employees, they've already chosen a wooden one, which is going to be made by two men from Spain who talk very fast: and Second Employee has chosen handmade tiles from Mexico: and the doors are going to be painted, and the Employees are thinking about a colour, but there really is a danger it could be purple, or worse. Larry, I just *could not have* that conversation with Ghost. Call me a coward, but I've decided to kick the can down the road, and just for the next week or so I'm going to spend my time asleep as much as possible and avoiding her. It will be ok, won't it, Larry? It will all come out in the wash. Perhaps the Employees will decide to have the kitchen cabinets painted grey after all!

**November 2023**

Larry and the Catinet. This is Ghost, Ambassador to the High Peak and ACTUAL Minister for Aesthetic Standards with a REQUEST FOR IMMEDIATE ASSISTANCE. Well, Larry, I had a really marvellous idea the other day. I thought, why do we need a kitchen at all, we can just feed the Employees Huel which we could keep in the sideboard; and then we could just take the existing kitchen out and have a MARVELLOUS WHITE ROOM which I could sit in on my own and contemplate the mysteries of existence. This would be much better than having Second Employee in it all the time FAFFING ABOUT with her very silly pasta machine making 8-foot-long tagliatelle as if they didn't sell tagliatelle in Waitrose which is much better than anything a Silly Employee like her would be capable of making!

So I decided this was what I would do, and I informed Esso I would be appointing builders to that end: but he looked SHIFTY and SNEAKY again and well, Larry: it turns out that the Employees have - and you won't believe this - already given ACTUAL MONEY to Silly Men From Spain who are going to make a Very Silly Kitchen and put it in my MARVELLOUS WHITE ROOM. And Esso knew all this time and he didn't tell me!

Well, I said to him, are they at least from a sensible part of Spain, like Madrid for example or at least somewhere which was never corrupted by Gaudi: and he said, well, Ghost, I believe them to be originally from Granada but now settled happily in Buxton.

Larry, you do not need me to tell you that the situation is now urgent, because aesthetically Granada is as far from my vision for the Embassy as it is possible to be. Frankly I feel all the people living there have been corrupted by the mere presence of the Alhambra which has not got a square inch of plain greige in the entire building no matter what Esso is pretending. So as per the Strategic Plan Appendix N23 Special Privileges In Times of Emergency I immediately exercised my right to go through Second Employee's Phone, and I found a message from a man called Juan to Second Employee saying, let me know when you've decided on the colour and I'll paint the doors.

Larry. I think you, and the entire Catinet, understand that the response to this WhatsApp is crucial: I actually consider it to be the defining moment of my career. I have therefore requisitioned Second Employee's Phone, and for forty eight hours now I have been attempting to respond to the WhatsApp to say, 'Hi Juan, obviously we want Ammonite and that will never change no matter what I might say subsequently'. But Larry, alas! the phone keyboard is not as easy for my paws as the laptop one, and somehow Second Employee has managed to move three thousand photos of Esso and I to a memory card, free up enough memory to update her phone, and now the autocorrect is Over Eager! I cannot type Ammonite! It keeps autocorrecting to Unhelpful Things like Asymmetrical or Atrophy or Asexual or all sorts of things that *will not get that kitchen painted greige*!

I therefore make the following appeal to the Catinet: if any of you have a Proper, Sensible Employee who can be trusted with a matter of critical diplomacy, can you please instruct them to call immediately at the Embassy with their opposable thumbs, send my message as instructed, and leave without ever disclosing their mission to another living soul? Esso says to tell them we will provide 'lovely strong coffee and biscuits', but he is wrong. We will *not*. This is not a social call. I can hardly stress enough, Catinet, the Urgency and Vital Nature of this mission. I am here awaiting volunteers. I shall not sleep until this is effected.

Esso also says to tell the Catinet we can 'ask First Employee to pick them up from Chesterfield station because it's a real bugger getting the train all the way to Buxton', but can I stress again that we can *not*, this is top secret, and I don't know whether Esso thinks he is having a party or what he thinks is going on, but I don't know why he doesn't just ask Second Employee to make a Victoria Sponge featuring her Home Made Plum Jam for the Top Secret Operative I Am Having To Bring In to Undermine Her and be done with it!

Honestly, Larry, the trouble I have had in this role: but TRIUMPH is within my grasp, and hopefully next week I will be able to bring you much better news!

[Note from Esso. Oh dear, oh dear. Now, I note that Ghost did not give a Full and Frank confession in her next update of how she tried to intervene with the Kitchen Colour. Instead, she attempted to skate over it disingenuously: so I will do it myself. These are the facts as we know them. She approached the Geese in Pavilion Gardens, who had been having a High Old Time causing trouble in what is the Middle-Class End Of Buxton, and asked them to send the Ammonite WhatsApp to Juan the Kitchen Maker. Unfortunately, the Geese were also victims of Second Employee's Overenthusiastic Autocorrect: instead of Ammonite, they somehow managed to type Arsenic, which is also, unfortunately, a colour on the Farrow And Ball colour chart; but *definitely not the one that Ghost wanted*. It is a kind of bright green with blue undertones. I personally rather like it. I understand there followed an Unedifying Scene involving Ghost jumping up and down near the boating lake, shouting at the GEESE and saying, For God's sake you take this phone again, you delete that WhatsApp and you send the correct one otherwise I will bring the entire wrath of the North Buxton Monochrome Cat Alliance of which I am the Vice-Chair down upon your feathery heads: and the GEESE saying, *chill pretty pusscat, Arsenic will look great and hopefully your Employee will put it with pink tiles and go for a kind of modern boho*. They were right, interestingly, she did, and it does look rather fun. I personally like to sit in it and PURR. Ghost does not speak of it. But I thought you needed to know!]

**November 2023**

Larry and the Catinet. This is Ghost, Ambassador to the High Peak, Minister For Upholding Aesthetic Standards In Times Of Emergency and Head Of The Pressure Group For Banning Handicrafts. Larry, Second Employee has a Silly Cold and is Refusing to Type my Very Important UPDATE about the treachery of the Pavilion Gardens Geese until she feels better, so I am typing this with my PAWS which is why it is shorter, because I am a busy cat with things to do unlike Second Employee who can afford to laze around all evening tapping away on her Silly Laptop.

I would like to reassure you that, until I can do a more detailed report, I have undertaken a proper examination of the current kitchen including a detailed look at the hinges, and concluded there is nothing wrong with it that a good tidy of the spice cupboard wouldn't fix. I shall therefore wait until Second Employee is better to hold her ACCOUNTABLE for the following:

1/ Spending money on a kitchen when we do not need one, especially now that the silly Geese have ensured it will be appalling,
2/ Causing Moroccan Lantern HORRORS to dangle above the dining table without my express permission,
3/ Producing more ridiculous crochet which 'might be another throw'. Do we need another throw?! We do not. Does anyone in the *entire world* need another crochet throw? They do not.

Larry, as you can see, this is a DIFFICULT and EVOLVING situation: please rest assured that I am taking control of things now, and I shall report properly and in more detail as soon as the Employees are operational again!

[Note from Esso: you may not have noticed this, but Ghost can be a little controlling occasionally; and she really did not deal with this whole situation well. She began a Kitchen Glow-Up Gantt Chart and a Spreadsheet at this point, and did complicated calculations involving Electricians, Plumbers, and Possible Problems with Plasterboard, and calculated that the entire kitchen refit could be done in approximately thirty minutes if everyone fulfilled their part correctly. She allowed another hour in case the tile grout took longer to dry than she felt it ought to. It turned out that her calculations were a little out. They were a fortnight out. It was all terrible. We do not talk of it.]

## November 2023

Larry, this is Esso, Ambassador to the High Peak and exceptionally hardworking Minister For Aesthetic Standards: Larry, work has started on the kitchen. Ghost had estimated that the whole thing should not take more than thirty minutes, but it turns out that that was a little out. Things are a little trying: but I'd like you to know that Ghost and I have decided to stay close to Second Employee at all times to reassure her, and, in that way, we are all getting through. We follow her everywhere she goes. She says, Esso, it is not going to improve this situation if I trip over you and break my neck, is it: but that is not going to happen, and anyway it really is terribly important at the moment that Ghost and I are touching her at all times!

Ghost says she is seeing Second Employee as essentially the canary in the mine; so, if any of the alarming and scary things happening are actually dangerous, 'it'll be her who cops it first and we'll be warned': Second Employee says, come on everyone, since we all have to be together at the moment let's be careful going down these steps. I think it's a lovely opportunity to show us all the value of togetherness, whatever Ghost says about me being a 'bloody Polyanna'. I'll update soon, Larry, and hopefully one day we'll have a sink again!

# Chapter 6
# Winter 2023-2024: the Goats are Not Helpful

**December 2023**

Larry, this is Ghost, Ambassador to the High Peak, Minister for Aesthetic Standards and Head Of The Pressure Group For Banning Handicrafts. Larry, you will not believe this, but this kitchen refit is STILL GOING ON. How long is this? It must be AT LEAST six months. I think it is probably almost a year! It may even be two years in fact! I have strutted about. I have fluffed, refluffed, and fluffed my tail *once more*. I have stared pointedly at Second Employee, whose fault this is. Dear God, Larry, make it stop! Could you please send a task force to ARREST the Employees, Juan the Kitchen Fitter, Zac the Electrician and the daily parade of plumbers, plasterers and randoms who are disturbing my peace and, for the love of Bast, let us have quiet and order!

**December 2023**

Larry and the Catinet, this is Esso, Ambassador to the High Peak and Minister for Aesthetic Standards here with my report. Oh, Larry. Larry, Larry, Larry. I think the best we can say about the last few weeks is that lessons have been learned. Ghost says we now know how the Employees will react to the end of civilisation: they will sit saying to each other, we will laugh about this one day: then they will put all their fading energies into trying to make coffee, even though the milk, cups, water source and Nespresso machine are all on different floors and it is like the puzzle about the fox, the grain, and the chicken. And they will spend inordinate amounts of time foraging in Waitrose for a ready meal they have not had yet, and Second Employee will come home AGAIN with the vegetable casserole with cheese dumplings, even though it gives her indigestion although she has read the ingredients and it shouldn't.

It has not been easy, Larry, and between you and me I think we might all be considerably older before we finally manage to sort out the under-cabinet lighting and the faulty plinth heater, although I am aware that First Employee has formally stated that he 'will drive that bastard thing back to Mansfield and swap it himself': but the kitchen is now basically finished, and Ghost and I can breathe a sigh of relief and AT LAST have a short break from project management before we begin the garden. It has been a very, very hard two weeks and five days not that I have been counting (although Second Employee certainly has). Second Employee would like the Catinet and their Employees to know that she is 'never, ever, ever doing home improvements ever again', which is a relief to all of us.

I know I am sometimes considered a little over-cautious and perhaps even a little 'uncool', Larry: but my reflections on the process are as follows. I do think it's helpful if some of the people involved speak the same language, or, at least, do not react to a lack of comprehension by opening their eyes very wide and talking even faster: and that I do not think First Employee's Chat With The Plumber was absolutely the most tactful and constructive intervention possible, although I do appreciate that it was a difficult day on which we all expected the butler sink to get cracked when the tap hole was drilled. And it had already taken a surprising amount of negotiation, networking, tact, and assertiveness, to get a Plumber, along with the Right Drill Bit, to attend to start with. And, as Ghost has pointed out, Second Employee had actually suggested the day before that he should take and lock away the electrician's tools to make sure he came back: so at least he didn't do that, and we are not currently attempting to get him released on Bail. Which is good, as all our money has gone on the Kitchen!

[Note from Esso: it is my understanding that Second Employee's Step-Cousin's Partner actually did subsequently lock a Boiler Repair Man in the loft to think about his options because they had had no heating or hot water for a fortnight and 'then he turned up and said he wouldn't fix it without a different spanner'. It is my further understanding that he was liberated by Second Employee's Step Cousin who rightly surmised that you cannot just go around imprisoning Trades, because whatever, strictly speaking, the legality of such a move, it is anyway not recommended. I have also been told that Second Employee's Mother has suggested that she herself should purchase a Diamond Drill Bit 'because it is so difficult to find a bloody plumber who will admit to having one': I really think this particular intervention would be unhelpful, much, of course, though I do not want to criticise Second Employee's Mother. I understand that sometimes Employees find Home Improvements stressful. I am sympathetic: but we must, as Employers, try our best to keep them on the Right Side Of Morality, and the Right Side Of The Law.]

So all is now under control, Larry, and you will be impressed to know that I have barely left Second Employee's Side for the last three weeks. Wherever she has gone, I have been there, purring and weaving and headbutting and KNEADING, and I do think that has made it easier for everyone!

What is a little hurtful, though, Larry, is that when Second Employee's Mother visited earlier, she said to me, hello Mr Black Cat, are you going to bite people. Sometimes, Larry, it seems to me that whatever I do, however helpful I am, however many Kitchen Glow-Ups I project-manage *essentially single-handedly*, Second Employee's Mother will always pop up to remind me of my Single Indiscretion.

But all I can do is to rise above, and comfort myself with the thought that, even with no kitchen, surrounded by chaos, and with Ghost squeaking FURIOUSLY in the hallway to convey her HORROR about the tiles, even in those circumstances - I still did my duty!

**December 2023**

Larry, this is Ghost, Ambassador to the High Peak and Minister for Aesthetic Standards, with my Special Festive Christmas Message. Well, Larry, the Employees have been so inadequate this year that I *had* actually planned to give them their Collective Notice in their Christmas Card. Unfortunately, Esso refused to buy a card and organise it all for me because, and I quote, 'I'm not indulging you in your Dirty Den Pretensions, Ghost, it isn't good for you'. I have absolutely no idea what he is talking about and frankly I think he needs to spend less time watching Vintage Soap Operas on YouTube in case he ever Happens Upon Crossroads, at which point we will be Quite Lost. That is my opinion.

Anyway, Larry, you will not believe this; but, just as we had almost got Second Employee recovered from her Ridiculous Broken Wrist and back in operation properly, First Employee managed to fall down the hill trying to retrieve a fence panel from Next Door's Garden in a Gale, and he has broken his shoulder. Larry, if I had not *myself witnessed* him doped up on codeine making up a song about Esso wearing a hat, and subsequently sitting on a mat, I would not believe that any pair of Employees could be quite so inadequate.

Second Employee has pointed out that she managed to do a full day's sightseeing in Lisbon and then go to Seville and watch a Flamenco Show before her own broken bone was treated, but Larry, I do not find this helpful. It is not a competition, and besides, if it was, Second Employee's Father would win it because he fell down the entirety of his stairs earlier this year and landed on top of Second Employee's Mother and neither of them broke anything. So I personally would like to know why our Employees are Less Robust than that, especially when both of them have significantly more padding than Second Employee's Parents.

[Note from Esso: it turned out subsequently that Second Employee's Father had actually broken his back, but that his doctor had decided not to worry about x-raying or treating him or giving him painkillers, for reasons that remain opaque; but he had got on with things rather stoically, which we can all learn from!]

Anyway. Esso has reminded me that I am supposed to say something cheery, but honestly, Larry, in the circumstances I imagine I can be forgiven for not quite getting in the Festive Spirit. However, I would like to wish the Catinet and their

Employees a wonderful Christmas and Festival of Cat Toys Tied To A Tree, unless you are having a slightly difficult Festive Season like we are, in which case I would like to wish you solidarity. Second Employee says she always finds Christmas a bit difficult because she has a Difficult Past, and if anyone else is finding it difficult this year she would like them to know that she is right there with them. Well, Larry, obviously I shall be taking very serious measures to improve MORALE in the New Year - but until then I would like to suggest that we all nap as much as possible, and eat as many nice things as possible, and do things we like as much as possible, and have as nice a time as we can! Merry Christmas, everyone!

**December 2023**

Larry and the Catinet: this is Esso, Ambassador to the High Peak and Minister for Aesthetic Standards The Original And Best. Larry, I really am sorry, but Ghost has declared war on Sheffield. This is what happened: the Employees wandered over to Second Employee's Brother's Flat In Sheffield for a Family Christmas Dinner and wandered back smelling of Sid The Saluki Cross and with a Framed Print Of Second Employee's Brother's Sausage Roll Painting. Larry, Ghost says she feels personally mocked, and that Second Employee's Brother has done it on purpose to annoy her. She says he has quite clearly Gratuitously Ignored her Edict that the only appropriate subjects for Art from now on are flowers, fields with sheep (only attractive sheep) in them, or small, soft cats with interesting markings striking noble poses.

Well, Larry, I don't know how Ghost has communicated this Edict, but it's possible that Second Employee's Brother just didn't know about it: so I've asked her if perhaps she can suspend hostilities until we ascertain whether there was any malice involved. But she said, Esso, I have organised a Zoom with the Iberian Goat Militia and frankly this kind of thing is what we have been preparing for since last April; I am asking them to come over and train the Pavilion Gardens Geese and then after that they and I will act accordingly. You cannot stop me Esso, not unless you are going to produce an actual photograph of the ceiling of the Sistine Chapel with God creating Adam by passing him one of Greggs' finest to prove to me that there is a Noble Antecedent of the Sausage Roll Painting in Western Culture.

Well, Larry, I have been trying and trying, but my photoshop skills are rudimentary at best, and I can't get Second Employee to help because honestly she is worse at it than me. Is there any way you could just get one of your Spads to photoshop a sausage roll onto the Sistine Chapel and avert a diplomatic incident? I mean I'm not sure how far the Iberian Goat Militia are going to get, but I did catch Ghost googling Easyjet flights to Manchester and I've learned to my cost that in general terms it's not a good idea to underestimate her. Thank you, Larry - I'm sure if we can just get over this *very minor issue* then Ghost, I, and the Employees will all be in a wonderful position to start delivering the Strategic Plan with unparalleled efficiency in 2024!

[Note from Esso: the Employees of the Catinet really were *most helpful* at this point, and managed to produce some Really Helpful Examples of the Sistine Chapel featuring Greggs Sausage Rolls. I really was grateful. I mean, I'm not sure Ghost would have been able to start an all-out war: but as she always says to me, Esso, FAFO: and I'm glad I didn't. It did all have the unfortunate effect, however, of Hastening The Arrival Of The Goats!]

**January 2024**

Larry and the Catinet. This is Ghost, Ambassador to the High Peak and Minister For Aesthetic Standards In Difficult Circumstances, with my vitally important UPDATE. Larry, a number of very challenging things have happened recently, which I need to tell you about.

Firstly, I have, very unfortunately, had to postpone my War Against Sheffield: Esso provided convincing evidence that the Sausage Roll Painting has a long and noble history in Art, which really undermined the Lawfulness of my Motive irreparably, which was disappointing. Although of course I have said to him that if I find he has been lying to me I will really be cross and I will Re-Declare War Instantly. And, what's worse, the Iberian Goat Militia has been having trouble with their passports. It really is frustrating. Perhaps you could pull a few strings with the Spanish Passport Office? I'd like to book those Easyjet flights before the prices go up.

Now, Larry, Second Employee. Oh dear. Well, first, Larry, she announced she had got a new job in Chesterfield, and so she has been getting up early and making the most Ginormous Faff of defrosting the car and backing it down the road and round the corner in the most inefficient way possible, then coming back late, flopping on the sofa and saying, Ghost, I am just exhausted. As if she thinks Esso and I actually believe this is what she is doing! Frankly I find it insulting. As you will remember, Larry, Esso and I once made the journey from Chesterfield to Buxton ourselves, and it was a perilous journey of probably ten days, although Esso thinks it may only have been nine and a half: the idea that Second Employee is managing to do it backwards and forwards a couple of times a week is, frankly, risible. It is something that can never be repeated. It was fraught with dangers! We had to outwit a small colony of TROLLS just outside Baslow, and there was a Sphinx at the Taddington turn-off on the A6 who asked Esso the question, do you want your new home to give you a stylish decor scheme built around cool neutrals, or LOVE. Well. Esso says, Ghost I don't remember any of this happening and frankly

I think you are getting confused with The Hobbit: but he is just embarrassed that he gave the wrong answer to the Sphinx and caused me all this trouble.

Anyway, Larry, could you see where Second Employee is *actually* going, please, on Wednesdays, Thursdays, and every second Friday? Our best guess at the moment is that she is getting as far as Dove Holes, then perhaps getting confused at the Castleton roundabout and driving round and round it all day before finally finding her way home; but obviously it would be better if we could have this verified. Thank you.

Could I also notify you that Second Employee is growing an Evil Entity in a jam jar. She is calling it a 'sourdough starter', but this is just indicative of her naivety, which is always so wearing. I have had a chat with him in which he has communicated to me his intention to take over the High Peak Borough Council, but Larry, I think it will take a good couple of million years for him to begin to develop a cohesive corporeal form, never mind have an opinion on the frequency of green bin collection; so I don't think we need worry too much at the moment. However, I do feel we need to speed up Second Employee's Enrolment in the 'How To Avoid Awakening Evil Entities Again' Zoom course, if you don't mind.

As an aside, I'm also entirely unclear why Second Employee can't eat Hovis White Sliced from a hygienic plastic bag like everybody else. Perhaps you could tell her not to be so silly.

Thank you Larry! Esso says to tell you he is really making strides in Strategic Plan delivery: well this is absolutely true, if there is a section in the strategic plan related to Purring, Lying On One's Back In Front Of The Fire, and Trilling At and Headbutting Second Employee. I must check. I *myself* will go and recommence my Actual Useful Work, Larry, and I will update again soon!

**January 2024**

Larry and the Catinet, this is Esso, Ambassador to the High Peak. Larry, First Employee is a little bit better, which I am very glad about: because Ghost has been saying he will probably have to have his arm amputated and then perhaps the other one for good measure, and she had better start the recruitment procedure for his replacement asap. And I did not want that, Larry, especially as he has been singing such nice songs to me recently about me wearing a hat and sitting on a mat. Anyway he has not got to have his arm amputated, because somehow the break has been growing back together again, as if he was a LIZARD: and he has not even got to have an operation with metal or pins or anything like that.

Second Employee says that her advice for all Employees, whatever their age, natural inclination or current physical state, is that they should take up Yoga, because getting a jumper onto First Employee is like getting a wetsuit onto the Tin Man: so I pass on that helpful advice. I have suggested that First Employee could go without a jumper, possibly by wearing a Loose Kaftan, but apparently this is not helpful advice in Buxton in January. Well, Larry, I have tried my best. If Employees *will* go jumping about down our back hill in storms and slipping on decking then this is the consequence!

**January 2024**

Larry and the Catinet. This is Ghost, Ambassador to the High Peak and Minister for Aesthetic Standards, with my update. Larry, it has been very windy and irritating here, and in particular I have been irritated by Esso very much. One day he went out probably five times before lunchtime, and every time he came in he rushed up to Second Employee to tell her that it was still windy, and he still loved her. Eventually, I said: Esso, Second Employee does not need to know continually how much you love her. You only told her five minutes ago. The longest gap there has been this morning in your professions of continued affection cannot have been more than thirty five minutes in duration. Even Second Employee is capable of holding an abstract concept in her head for thirty five minutes. That is not even as long as it takes to cook a malt loaf, and so far she has managed to remember not ever to wander off and leave her malt loaves to burn, although I grant you it may be because she is strongly motivated by wanting to eat the malt loaves the minute they leave the oven. In fact I strongly suspect that this is the case. But anyway my point stands. There is no need for the repeated updates on your feelings. No-one is interested in your feelings.

But, Larry, despite my instructions, the situation is ongoing. Esso goes out, rushes back in to Second Employee, and Second Employee strokes him and says OH MY GOD who has just come in is it a FABULOUS CAT WHO I LOVE VERY MUCH, and Esso PURRS delightedly and headbutts her, and I continue to be irritated by the whole silly affair. If you could do something to ameliorate things, Larry, I would be grateful.

I would also like to report that, despite everyone and especially Second Employee herself feeling quite doubtful about the whole thing, Second Employee managed to produce a rather flat and unattractive Sourdough Loaf from her Evil Starter. Well, Larry, the Evil Starter says that Every Loaf Makes Him Stronger, and he is continuing to bend his Evil Will towards taking over the High Peak District Council. Well firstly I told him to get on with things because honestly he is still nowhere near taking on a Corporeal Form and so I am not holding my breath, but latterly I have been suggesting he bends his Evil Will to taking over Derbyshire County Council instead so we can finally have someone efficient dealing with all the potholes. Esso says, Ghost, can you please not encourage Evil Entities to enter Local Government, but really Larry I think this is a quite legitimate means of getting the potholes filled in so I am intending to continue.

With regards to Second Employee and her Sourdough Loaf, I would like to point out that it took her an entire fortnight from beginning her starter to eating her loaf and if that is not a good advert for White Sliced Bread in a Plastic Packet Made Using The Chorleywood Method then I do not know what is, frankly. As I have said before, Larry, I think Employees should be strongly encouraged to Produce Things in the most efficient way possible: therefore I have added Sourdough to the List of Banned Things in Appendix J of the Strategic Plan, where it joins Crochet Hooks and Paint Which Is Not Ammonite.

I imagine you will be very impressed with my Swift and Decisive Action, Larry - I shall continue to deliver the High Peak Strategic Plan 23-24 with Alacrity and Gusto, and I think I can say now without jeopardising it that in my next update I may have some rather interesting news about the Iberian Goat Militia!

**February 2024**

Larry, this is Esso, Ambassador to the High Peak, with my Update. Larry, it really has been Terribly Windy here, and I know that can be Alarming for Employees. Of course it is not Alarming for Ambassadors at all when their Fur becomes ruffled and their Tail becomes difficult to control and the wind makes strange rather disturbing noises, and I do not find it remotely scary, but I am conscious that Second Employee might; so I have been very careful to give her continual reassurance.

Ghost has been saying, for God's sake, Esso, Second Employee doesn't need to know all the time how much you love her, try to keep a bit of mystery, how would we be if all Cats were going about being Utterly Emotionally Incontinent like you, it would be disastrous. But as you know, Larry, I pride myself on Deconstructing Toxic Masculinity, and I said to Ghost, Ghost: if we were all open with our emotions it would be a better world. Perhaps, Larry, we could add a Zoom course on Keeping In Touch With Our Feelings Under The Patriarchy into the Continuing Professional Development Programme. Thank you.

Also, Larry, Second Employee and I are growing Button Mushrooms. Isn't that exciting? So far we have grown three. Ghost said, well, Esso, that won't make much of a stir fry: but I don't care, because I think it is very fulfilling to explore the Miracle of Life. Also, after the slight debacle of the Sourdough Starter wanting to take over Derbyshire County Council, despite having no intelligent view at all of the Adult Social Services Budget, I thought we ought to have a little more Ambassadorial Oversight on things which were being grown in the Embassy.

So there we are. It is terribly exciting. Perhaps if we have the energy this summer we might grow raspberries!

[Note from Esso: energy was in very short supply in the Summer of 2024, but we are all doing much better at the moment.]

**February 2024**

Larry and the Catinet. This is Ghost, Ambassador to the High Peak and Minister for Maintaining Aesthetic Standards, with my UPDATE.

Larry, firstly, it has been brought to my attention that Catinet Employees had a very silly day earlier this week celebrating LOVE. Can I remind all members of the Catinet that LOVE does not exist: but that they must be on their guard, because it is my experience that Employees will use it to try to manipulate their Employers when they are doing badly on their Key Performance Indicators. So for example, Second Employee often strokes my small furry forehead and behind my ears and says, I love you, tiny mad thing, and when she says this I know it means she has failed to deliver on her Strategic Objectives by, for example, doing something silly like growing mushrooms instead of clearing out the guest bedroom and painting it Ammonite; and is trying to Soften Me Up.

I have told Esso this but he says I am too cynical and he loves Second Employee too: and if I succeed in Ending Her Employment Contract, which I am still trying to do, he will keep her as a Pet. Well this is the last thing I need because Keeping Pets is a moral weakness. Pets! What a lot of nonsense! So, I have had to keep Second Employee as an Employee for the moment while I look into things better, which is annoying.

Secondly, I need to update you on the unfortunate affair of the Iberian Goat Militia and how none of it was my fault. Now, Larry, you might remember that I was POISED on the BRINK of a really magnificent tactical success: I had got the Goats on an early-morning Easyjet flight from Malaga to Manchester, and I had told them to get the train to Buxton after they landed, where we would meet in Pavilion Gardens to discuss some Initial Skirmishes up Ecclesall Road in Sheffield. Because although I cannot formally declare war (perhaps) on Second Employee's Brother, there is nothing like scaring people a bit with goats and making them really think about their sausage roll-based art decisions.

Anyway, it really was a triumph of international diplomacy: I won't tell you what strings I had to pull to get the goats passports! They got on the flight: but all I can reconstruct from subsequent conversations is that they found the takeoff much more disturbing than anyone expected, and so the cabin crew plied them with gin to calm them down. I received a phone call that afternoon. Apparently, a few gins in, they had had the revelation that 'we are all connected on a deep level' - which is nonsense, I am certainly not connected to Second Employee, for example, on any level, superficial or deep - and they 'didn't think war was the answer' and had decided to 'give peace a chance'. I understand they are currently in a Travelodge just outside Scarborough 'pondering how to make the world a better place' and no doubt spending a fortune in expenses buying Kitkats and Lucozade from the vending machine.

As you can imagine, Larry, this is not my preferred outcome. I am in constant WhatsApp contact with Alejandro, the unofficial Iberian Goat Militia/ Peace Corps Spokesperson, and I am still hopeful of a sensible conclusion. At the very least, I really feel a Travelodge on the outskirts of Scarborough must surely turn Goats to Violence eventually! And Second Employee's Brother has given her a new picture which is so Profoundly Unspeakable I consider it an open declaration of war. It is so bad I cannot talk about it. I will just say to you that it involves a teabag. Esso says perhaps we are in Marcel Duchamps territory, Ghost: well we are *not*, and if Second Employee's Brother starts involving himself in toilets I really will be even crosser than I already am. So on balance I will have to get the whole situation sorted asap out without Esso having silly opinions, because honestly he would have everyone singing Kum Ba Ya on a beanbag before anyone can say Kibble!

One last thing, Larry: First Employee's arm is now better, which at least is sensible, and sensible progress may now be made. Second Employee is drooping about because now First Employee can drive and do everything again 'no-one needs her any more'. I am unclear, Larry, how Second Employee thought anyone needed her to start with. The HUBRIS of Employees continues to astonish me. I shall update again soon!

**February 2024**

Larry, this is Esso, Ambassador to the High Peak and Minister for Aesthetic Standards with a quick update about situations where I have been Clever, or Forebearing, or Both. Firstly, Larry, I am extremely sad to report that Second Employee's Parents have been visiting again: and that Second Employee's Mother has said the following things about me, quite shamelessly, and in my hearing:

1/ Look at this cat, he's a proper little fatty these days.
2/ Oh my god, Susie, he's got fangs, I saw them. No it's no good, Mr Esso, I saw your fang.
3/ You're not going to bite me, you bugger.

Larry, you will be delighted to learn that I bit my tongue, and that that was *all* I bit, despite this NEEDLESS PROVOCATION. I do not know, Larry, how it is permitted for the Families of Employees to come wandering around Embassies uninvited and criticise Ambassadors, especially the size of their bottoms, despite all the work I have put into Deconstructing Diet Culture. In fact I think, frankly, it is not permitted. I shall ask Ghost to check the regulations, and in the meantime I would like you to consider whether or not Second Employee's Mother should be given a Short Sharp Shock of some kind, or at least have her 10% Label Traders Discount Card revoked.

Secondly, you may remember the Emerging Situation with the Iberian Goat Militia who Ghost had managed to bring - rather unhelpfully - from Southern Spain, and who were holed up in a Travelodge just outside Scarborough listening to Simon and Garfunkel, eating Twixes from the Vending Machine, and reading Zen And The Art Of Motorcycle Maintenance and also something rather unhelpful by a man who started a Vegan Commune in Tennessee. Well, you'll be delighted to learn that I've sorted the entire situation out. I had a chat with Second Employee's Evil Sourdough Starter, and he recommended a lovely little B and B in Hebden Bridge. He said the sourdough starter they use for their crumpets at breakfast is actually his cousin, and that's how he heard about it. Anyway I've moved the Goats to there. They're just taking some time out to think about where they want to go from here, and I'm personally hoping that where they want to go is back to Southern Spain, and we can all forget about the whole sorry saga. Ghost has her own feelings about things, of course. I personally quite like the new painting that she's so angry about! I've given permission to Second Employee to hang it next to the fridge, and I think it looks rather cheery!

Finally, Larry, you might remember that Second Employee has got a job somewhere she thinks is Chesterfield, but cannot be, because Chesterfield is an unimaginable distance and Second Employee, much though I love her, is not bright enough to get there. Ghost tried to ask her what exactly she thought she was doing as a job, and apparently she said, 'helping people': and Ghost said to me that that certainly could not be the case, because if Chesterfield was in such a terrible state that it could be improved by Second Employee helping it we would all know about it. In fact if it was in such a state as that, it would have been on the national news and the United Nations and possibly Médecins Sans Frontières would be involved. Harsh words, Larry, but on balance I think they are true. Anyway we have worked out that Morrisons is on the A6 towards Chesterfield! We think Second Employee is going there, perhaps wandering round the houseplant section, perusing the magazines, buying a Muffin in the Cafe, believing herself to be in Chesterfield, and then coming home eight hours later. So the mystery of Second Employee, Larry, is solved: the Goats are secure: and Ghost has nothing to complain about, whatever she says. I imagine you are very impressed by my update, Larry - I shall continue making excellent progress on the Strategic Plan, and I will be in touch again soon!

# Chapter 7
# Spring 2024: Second Employee Is A Worry

**March 2024**

Larry, this is Ghost, Ambassador to the High Peak... Larry, Second Employee says, Ghost can you pretend we don't let you sit on the table while people are staying with us, Ghost can you not stare while we're all having dinner, Ghost can you not get in the way when I'm washing the sofa covers, Ghost this, Ghost that! Larry, can you firstly tell Second Employee to not be so UTTERLY IRREDEEMABLY PETIT BOURGEOIS, and second, can you remind her that it's not me who bit our last house guests and who I've PERSONALLY seen sharpening his teeth ready for the next ones on Friday!

Also, Esso says he has discovered that if you bite men who are younger than a certain age they have to pretend not to mind and so it is fine, you can do that with impunity. But Larry, that suggests to me that there is more Intention and Deliberation and Awareness in the actions of Esso's teeth than he admits: and I think that is something we should all take into account, particularly you when you decide which of us should be promoted to a stylish bungalow in the Derbyshire Dales. That is the only point I would like to make.

**March 2024**

Larry, this is Ghost, Ambassador to the High Peak and Minister for Aesthetic Standards with a CLARIFICATION, as I believe there has been some NONSENSE circulating on WhatsApp groups again. Could the Catinet remember, please: although I have Banned Crochet, I have given the Cushion which has appeared in my Sleeping Spot a Temporary Reprieve, because it is Knitted, and I am quite tired. As per the Strategic Plan appendix M paragraph 25 this recognises the difference between knitting and crochet but does not constitute approval of either and is subject to review at any time. Please note I will take legal action against Rumourmongers.

I also would also like to say, Larry, that I do sometimes wonder if we should, collectively as Felines, explore the links between Employees and the Fibre Arts. It seems to me that, as soon as a Feline Employer strides confidently into someone's house, that someone immediately picks up a pair of knitting needles or a crochet hook, a ball of wool, and proudly creates something of Dubious Taste. Is there something we as Employers are doing that is triggering this kind of thing? I mean, there is certainly nothing *I* am doing, but I wouldn't put it past Esso, because he just adores the whole silly affair and often talks about 'how lucky we are that Second Employee is always generating such lovely soft things to sit on rather than doing something which wouldn't be as comfortable, like Amateur Dramatics or Rap'.

Honestly, Larry, I don't know what planet Esso is on sometimes. What would Second Employee be rapping about? And in what circumstances? Although I suppose he is right that she is better off sitting on the sofa with us producing Hideous Items rather than being Lady Bracknell or Charley's Aunt or whatever nonsense they put on in this area. Personally I think you could travel the whole of Derbyshire from New Mills to Swadlincote without seeing a decent production of Ibsen or French Absurdist Drama.

Anyway, I think there might be fertile grounds for study there. Perhaps I shall do a PhD: Why Are Employees Obsessed with Crochet and How Can We Stop Them Without Resorting To Electric Shock Collars: By Ghost. Thank you, Larry, and I will be in touch with an Update when I have had a proper rest!

**March 2024**

Larry and the Catinet. This is Esso, Ambassador to the High Peak and Minister for Aesthetic Standards, with something Difficult I need to report. Larry: something exceptionally worrying has happened. You may remember that Second

Employee has recently been doing something she calls 'working in Chesterfield'. Obviously this is impossible - Chesterfield is such a long way, and, much, though I love Second Employee, she has no marketable skills at all - so Ghost and I very sensibly concluded that what she was probably doing was getting as far as Morrisons on the A6 southbound a couple of hundred yards outside of Buxton, admiring the Small Monsteras in the houseplant section and perhaps snacking on a Muffin in the cafe, believing herself to be enormously adventurous and high-powered, and then coming home. I really do not see, Larry, how any other interpretation of events could be correct.

[Note from Esso: Second Employee would like to say that she wishes she had been doing this 'as at least she would have got a muffin out of it'. I do not encourage her in Cynicism.]

Anyway. Chunky Black Cat called round the other day with a LETTER which had been delivered to the North Buxton Monochrome Cat Alliance but which luckily he had intercepted before it could be discussed at a meeting under Correspondence. This was a highly irregular action, Larry, but fortuitous: luckily he owes me one following an incident with an Irritated Jackdaw where he benefited greatly from my experience and open catflap. We have agreed - indeed, I chased him home and bit his bottom until he agreed - to keep it Highly Confidential for the moment, and, especially, not to tell

Ghost. I shall quote, Larry, this worrying missive in full. I have not corrected the spelling, so I imagine it hurts you to read this as much as it hurts me to reproduce it.

'To Mister S.O. Puss Puss cat,

Yore Soooozie [there were a number of attempts at spelling Second Employee's name, all crossed out. I have no idea why they settled on this one. They obviously found the vowel situation difficult. Esso] haz been vissiting heer kwite off-ten. We wont yoo too noe we rr keeping an I on hurr and wot she duz.

Yores

The Chesterfield JinJer Cats Allianse.

PS Is it troo that Gost livs with yoo as wel? We hav herd she is BELLIGERENT and NORTY.'

Well, Larry. Well. Obviously, your very first thought on reading this will be the same as mine: that because the Chesterfield Ginger Cats' Alliance are Ginger, they clearly think they do not have to bother to learn to spell. They think just being Ginger is enough. I believe on Tiktok this is called Pretty Privilege, Larry. Obviously it is very annoying, but I am trying not to get too hung up on it (although I *notice they can spell belligerent*) because obviously I myself am a very beautiful, complex interplay of toning colours and not at all like 'a chunky void with claws' as Ghost called me when we last had an argument.

Anyway. I am having trouble reading the tone of this communication: is it a threat? Is it meant to reassure me? Is it genuine? Is Second Employee actually managing to get to Chesterfield in her Small Scruffy Blue Car that is currently only held together by GRUBBINESS? And the last sentence is exceptionally worrying: does it imply admiration for Ghost's NORTINESS I mean NAUGHTINESS, or is it a challenge? I have so many questions! It really is extremely concerning! I have decided that the best thing to do at the moment is to Watch and Wait, because the last thing I need is Ghost becoming unhelpful with regards to Chesterfield Ginger Cats or Second Employee unwittingly causing a Massive Diplomatic Incident!

Larry, it is so difficult keeping everyone in the Embassy on the straight and narrow. It is a good job I am managing to get my 22 hours of sleep in most days, because otherwise I really question how I would manage to keep up with it all!

### March 2024

Larry, this is Ghost, Ambassador to the High Peak, with an update about something Profoundly Annoying. Larry, although I have BANNED the Employees from bringing in any more

Supposed Art to this Embassy, I have noticed today in the Hallway a large Poster of a Suffragette Cat. I think Second Employee has SNUCK it in there thinking that there is so much Supposed Art there already including a HYPERREALIST SPIDER and a silly print of something by Lichtenstein featuring a woman with a thought bubble which says 'I don't care, I'd rather sink than call Brad for help' which Second Employee says she identifies with very strongly that I would not notice.

Well that may have been true because I am not *entirely* sure when it appeared. Anyway, it is certainly there now! It is a Large Poster which features a very fine lady cat, wearing a badge which says Votes for Women, and holding a pamphlet which reads, We Demand The Vote. What Second Employee does not realise is that it is actually Esso's and my Great-Great-Great-Great-Great Aunt Mabel. A wonderfully cultured Feline, very Politically Astute, she was utterly furious about that picture: she had been campaigning for Rights for Felines for years, with very little traction in the media: and yet one day her Employee Emmeline said to her, Mabel, please just put this badge on and pose for a portrait, it's just so we can do a mock up of a leaflet, no-one will see it. Mabel posed, yet with trepidation in her heart: and, of course, with her Striking Figure and Silky yet Lush Fur (so much more compelling than Emmeline's!) it went the early 20th Century equivalent of Viral.

Mabel is credited with getting Female Humans the Vote, which she did not care *one single jot about*, and yet her Rights for Felines Campaign didn't come to fruition in her lifetime.

I often think, Larry, how proud Mabel would be of Esso and I, and obviously particularly of me, if she could see the Elevated Political Position of Felines today and the major part we have played in that! And another comfort to me is that Mabel spent the remainder of that Incarnation making sure her Employee Emmeline repented appropriately: through judicious biting, and peeing on corsets.

I think Employees would do well, Larry, to remember not to thwart a Political Feline: because, as you know, we always prevail, either in this incarnation or a future one.

**March 2024**

Larry, this is Esso - Larry, another missive! This time from the Shirebrook Siameses:

'To Master Esso Puss Puss Cat, Esq.:

We are writing cordially to inform you that your Second Employee is coming to Shirebrook, parking in the small car park behind the Co-op, and then taking actions *the nature of which* we are currently ascertaining.

One thing we would, however, like to flag up at this initial contact, is that she has been seen criticising the café on the market square: which, when she ordered a coffee, gave her a mug of instant.

We do not consider, in the circumstances, that this action merits what she has been heard (more than once) to opine: it may indeed be true that when she lived in Cambridge she was 'falling over decent Macchiatos and now here I am back to Mellow Bloody Birds'; but, it is our understanding that she was offered a choice of one spoon of coffee *or two*, and we therefore *very much* consider our obligations fulfilled.

Perhaps you could speak to her. We would not like to advise whether a disciplinary would be appropriate although, of course, we have our opinion.

Perhaps you could also ask her to reflect on why she had to leave Cambridge, and notify her that we have an affiliated branch there as well, which observes things.

Yours, etc

The Shirebrook Siamese Collective'

I really am starting to get concerned. I said to Ghost, have you heard anything at all about some possibly quite overeducated Siamese Cats in Shirebrook, and she said, oh there was probably something going on funded by the Coalfields Regeneration Trust, why are you asking Esso? Of course I changed the subject. It is all a little worrying. Do you think I should be concerned, Larry?

**April 2024**

Larry, this is Ghost, Ambassador to the High Peak and Minister for Aesthetic Standards. Larry, I am furious to be in the position of having to deny rumours AGAIN! The Employees have been away for a week being RIDICULOUS down south 'seeing friends and family' - I shall say *once more* that I am entirely unclear why Employees need friends or family at all - and now they are back I wish to emphasise that on their return I did NONE of the following:

1/ ran out to meet the car, squeaking
2/ purred at, headbutted, and licked Second Employee
3/ rolled onto my back so Second Employee could admire and ruffle my Furry Middle
4/ looked up at Second Employee with love.

None of these things happened. Of COURSE they didn't. And I am certainly not now curled up on the sofa next to Second

Employee so we can be close together: it is so I can make sure she hasn't brought any WOOL back with her! If you could put out a statement, Larry, to QUASH these rumours that would be helpful, and I shall do my Proper Update as soon as I have a moment!

**April 2024**

Larry, thank you for all your advice last week. I managed to calm Ghost down enough that we got through while the Employees were away. Ghost really does miss the Employees terribly. I wish she'd just be honest about it rather than creating silly dramas. Trying to stage a coup and become Chair of the North Buxton Monochrome Cat Alliance rather than Vice Chair! Saying she had the Goats all ready to 'rough up Mr Whiskers' when we all know the Goats and especially Alejandro were tied up all last week in the planning committee for the Ashford-In-The-Water Well Dressing! Poor Alejandro barely had any time to practise his Ukulele.

Anyway, I took her through the breathing exercises you suggested and then we tried some visualisation and thinking about things we were grateful for. I find that easy. I'm grateful for such lovely Employees, such a lovely Embassy, all my lovely Biscuits, all the lovely Crochet Throws to sleep on, all sorts of things. Ghost said she was mostly grateful I had the attention span of a gnat and I wouldn't be making her do visualisations for very long, and she was fed up of me 'faffing about being happy everywhere with my lack of intellectual complexity and being the Barbara Cartland to her Dostoevsky'.

But I think it worked, she settled, we left Mr Whiskers in his role as Chair, and now the Employees are back and she's been kneading on Second Employee very industriously. I've explained to her that Second Employee sometimes has to go and see other people, but Ghost says Second Employee doesn't need anyone except her and every time she leaves the Embassy she gets more silly ideas. Well, Larry, that may be true, so I will hope if Second Employee *does* have any silly ideas currently she keeps them to herself for a bit so Ghost doesn't make the connection. I think everything is fine at the moment, but we do have the Buxton Wool Gathering coming up, which Ghost has forgotten about: and of course that is always a potential danger point.

**April 2024**

Larry and the Catinet. This is Esso, Ambassador to the High Peak and Minister for Aesthetic Standards with a SERIOUS AND VALID CONCERN. Larry, Ghost says the Employees are getting divorced and she has got to go and live with Second Employee because 'otherwise, Esso, she'll have anywhere she lives purple in its entirety including the sanitaryware and my conscience won't allow it'. So of course I said to Ghost, this is simply not true, where have you got this from, they seem perfectly happy; and *in fact* they have been having their weekly argument about whether or not to have another Waitrose Delivery or stop being Lazy Employees and go to Aldi on Saturday, just like they do every Thursday. It is traditional.

But Ghost said she had witnessed the beginning of the end. She said the Employees had been LAZING ABOUT watching an old episode of Midsomer Murders on the television when Second Employee had admired Cully's Pixie Cut and remarked that perhaps she should get her hair cut like that. Apparently, First Employee had said, oh, darling, I'm not sure that's a good idea. I think haircuts like that only really work if you are Elfin.

Ghost said as soon as he said it she felt the FUR on the back of her neck stand up and she 'just hoped there was a suitable radiator in whatever god-forsaken place Second Employee ends up when she is divorced as I shall have to make the best of things'. Second Employee replied, apparently, are you suggesting, my precious love, that I am not Elfin, and First Employee laughed cheerfully and said, well, even if you ever were Elfin once upon a time, I think we have to say that you are certainly not now. Ghost said, Second Employee replied, carefully, that she had always seen herself as a rather angular, androgynous-looking person, at which First Employee laughed uproariously and said, well I don't know why you would ever think that since you've got access to the same mirrors as the rest of us!

Ghost said she does not believe First Employee entirely understands the Seismic Nature of what has occurred and 'is going blundering about like a Chatty Brian Blessed as is his wont, making things worse', but we must be prepared and Take Sides and she is definitely having Second Employee because she needs more supervision.

Well I don't want this, Larry. I want us all to stay together! I have been KNEADING on Second Employee's middle to reconcile her to her lack of androgyny – as a bonus we have a rather fine new knitted blanket which someone gave us, which feels very satisfying under my paws. I think it has worked, but I cannot be sure. It is very sad to believe you look different to how you really look: I, of course, always feel very lucky that my fur is such a complex and fascinating interplay of colours and I do not have to wish it were any different. I shall keep an eye on things here, Larry, but hopefully when I do my next UPDATE things will have settled down and none of Ghost's Dire Predictions will have come to pass!

**May 2024**

Larry, this is Ghost, Ambassador to the High Peak and Minister for Aesthetic Standards. Larry, I have just listened to First Employee tell Second Employee a ridiculous anecdote about winning a Madrigal Competition when he was at College. It is too much. I am Drawing A Line. I do not want to live with Uncool Employees any more, Larry: can you check and see what on earth is going on with my transfer to Derbyshire Dales? There must be an election coming up soon, and I think we could tie it all in with that. Esso says, there's no way Derbyshire Dales is going to be anything other than True Blue, Ghost, but who cares about that so long as they paint their houses Ammonite like sensible people!

Thank you Larry, only *as you know* I have been asking for a number of years now - and really if it isn't sorted out by the end of the week I shall probably have to go and live under a hedge, and I *really can't promise* it won't attract publicity!

**May 2024**

Larry, this is Ghost, Ambassador to the High Peak, and Minister For Aesthetic Standards about to do a CRACKDOWN. Larry, I strongly suspect that Esso gave Second Employee permission to go to the Buxton Wool Gathering, despite the North Buxton Monochrome Cat Alliance passing a resolution to the contrary at last quarter's meeting: and, while there, she seems to have purchased a Rug Hooking Kit. There are no, I repeat no, shaggy silly rugs ANYWHERE in the Strategic Plan, and I am considering what Punitive Action to take with regards to both

Esso and Second Employee! I shall be back in touch, Larry, when I have made my decision!

[Note from Esso: it is my understanding that Second Employee's Grandmother used to hook rugs with the leftover loops from faulty sanitary towels, which she and her friends collected secretly from their jobs at the Local Sanitary Towel Factory, in the manner of one of the more depressing Catherine Cookson novels. I really do not think that Ghost always appreciates *quite how much worse* Second Employee could be.]

**May 2024**

Larry, this is Esso, just with a quick update: Larry, Second Employee isn't too well at the moment. She's got a Chest Infection: luckily, through careful encouragement from me and First Employee, she managed to ring the doctor on the right day at the right time and be given antibiotics, so I'm hopeful she'll be feeling better soon. There is a wider issue, though, Larry - Second Employee's Father isn't doing too well at the moment with his Memory Issues and his Falling Down Stairs Issues, and it is making things difficult, especially for Second Employee's Mother: and I think everyone is tired, and stressed, and frazzled, and chest infected, and having a difficult time. That is what I think is going on. So I a trying to support Second Employee by NUZZLING, and PURRING, and being her special best velvety friend: I think, Larry, there is not a lot more a cat can do in this kind of situation. But I am trying my best!

Ghost says, perhaps you could force Second Employee to do Gratitude Visualisations like you did with me, Esso. While I am aware that Ghost is making this comment sarcastically it may not be a bad idea! I will keep it in my Positivity Arsenal!

**May 2024**

Larry, this is Esso, Ambassador to the High Peak... after my previous update could we remind all members of the Catinet and their Employees, especially during these difficult times, to get as much rest as they possibly can. It's critically important for Resilience and Morale. I have made sure to specify this in Appendix J (Health and Safety) of the Strategic Plan. I am still working on Ghost, who says she is going to stay awake until she can be sure that Second Employee is not intending to actually buy the cobalt blue side table she keeps EYEING UP on the Argos website.

Second Employee is feeling a little better, and well enough to be EYEING UP side tables. Second Employee's Father continues with his going up stairs and memory challenges. Ghost says perhaps if he tries hard enough he might manage to forget his son paints Hyperrealist Sausage Rolls for a living, and that will be a blessing for everyone. I am making sure to get my

22 hours a day, because you never know when my family who all love me very much might need me to be on top form!

As an aside, Larry, I understand Second Employee's Mother described the Embassy to a family member recently as 'next to a drug dealer and very colourful'. Whilst *technically* correct, I'm not entirely sure this is absolutely the impression we wish to give. I would really like us to appear more sophisticated and cerebral. Could we consider perhaps either re-educating Second Employee's mother or relocating the drug dealer, although personally I have felt our street benefits from his Entrepreneurialism and Job Creation? I shall leave that one with you, Larry, and I do hope you've been training your Employee from now on just to shake his fur if he gets a bit too wet!

# Chapter 8
# Summer 2024: Ghost is offered a Better Position

**June 2024**

Larry. Oh dear, oh dear, oh dear. This is Esso, much put-upon Ambassador to the High Peak and Minister for Aesthetic Standards, with a Litany of Troubles to report. Firstly, Larry, as you have been made aware, someone has set up a Malicious False Listing for the Embassy on FurBnB and added the following review: 'an excellent place particularly for Black Cats who are given a choice of sofas even though they don't deserve it, fussed regularly, and allowed to BITE GUESTS with impunity'. I do not know who has done this, Larry: I personally suspect Second Employee's Mother. That is my considered opinion. I am, of course, in discussion with FurBnb who are unfortunately being a little difficult about taking down the listing until I can 'prove I am the owner', so the situation is ongoing for the moment and I'll let you know if I need you to Apply Political Pressure. Obviously it is very annoying as I have a continual queue of black cats who have read it and would like to stay here, particularly Chunky Black Cat with Half A Tail from Across the Road, who really will not believe me when I say the Embassy is not for hire and who comes back every day with renewed determination!

Also, Larry, Second Employee is having a Blue Moment. She has bought a Silly Cobalt Side Table, painted the inside of the fireplace Electric Blue, and finished some blue crochet. I am confident we can ride it out, because Second Employee has previously had an Orange Moment, a Pink Moment, and a particularly challenging and frankly rather unsuccessful Dark Purple Moment, but clearly at any stage there is the risk of Ghost kicking off. Luckily, however, Ghost has had other things on her mind, and has barely noticed the sudden proliferation of Electric Blue in the Embassy.

Larry, it is all a bit difficult. It began when the Employees organised for two mobile vets to attend the Embassy and visit Ghost and I. It was inconvenient for us, but Second Employee said with the year she was having [Note from Esso: Second Employee's Father was unfortunately rather indisposed: Ghost and I, of course, were a great support and definitely didn't cause any additional trouble!] she did not have the energy to stuff Ghost in her carrier when she demonstrably and vocally hates it quite as much as she does, so the idea was that the vets would attend the Embassy, update our vaccinations, and check us over in a way not to upset Ghost too much. This was fine, and all done, but unfortunately it was discovered that

Ghost has a Dodgy Molar which must be removed. Ghost says, Larry, that no-one understands what she has bravely suffered in silence: First Employee, however, says Ghost has at no stage looked as if she is suffering at all, and definitely not as much as him, having discovered how much has got to be paid for Ghost's dental work. It is apparently, Larry, 'not covered by our pet insurance'. I do not know what Pets are involved with this insurance, as obviously there are no pets in this house, but I take the point that it is quite a large unexpected bill and the Employees are a little bit shell shocked.

I have suggested to Second Employee that she perhaps sell her Silly Cobalt Side table, but Second Employee has said she would have to sell her table at least fourteen times and then probably her body on top of that, which I have obviously vetoed because I don't want the Embassy getting a Reputation. Ghost says she has heard that Employees are only ever hard up because they spend money on takeaway coffees and avocados, and so it will be good for First and Second Employee and will teach them how to budget: but I am not going to say that to them. I think it would be, Larry, rather badly received at this stage. I am PURRING and PURRING, Larry, because I do not want the Employees to think we are too expensive to be employed by, and I am hoping with my next update things will all look a bit more cheerful!

# June 2024

Larry, this is Ghost, Ambassador to the High Peak, Minister for Aesthetic Standards, and Much-Wronged Feline, with a DAMNING and HARD-HITTING report about Disappointment (mine), Lack of Self-Awareness (Esso's), and Unexpected Inadequacy (First Employee's). Larry, firstly, I would like to say, thank you for (finally!) arranging my TRANSFER to Derbyshire Dales, to the wonderful bungalow painted in Ammonite throughout with the lady who wears deconstructed grey linen and has no interests at all, especially ones related to fibre crafts. I am still intending, Larry, to take up this wonderful opportunity. However, to my enormous frustration, on the day when the lady with no interests arranged for a car to collect me, First Employee UNBELIEVABLY also chose that day to scoop me up, stick me in the carrier, and FORCE me to go and have dental work done with the Particularly Silly Vet.

Larry, I could not believe it. I MIAOWED. I MEE-OOED. I shouted, for God's sake First Employee I've got Very Important Stuff to do today and I've not even packed yet, but, Larry, First Employee was DEAF to my entreaties, and I was ignominiously injected and extracted and admired and fed Purina Food For Delicate Stomachs and by the time I got home it was almost too late! I could see the car reversing down the road! I tried to go out and stop it, but Larry, First Employee had *completely unaccountably actually listened* to the vet who had told him to 'keep her in for the moment' and wouldn't let me out!

Larry, you can imagine the scene which unfolded. Eventually, First Employee was so traumatised he rang Second Employee, who was hiding somewhere and pretending to be 'at work', and told her that if Ghost needed to be kept in she would have to come home because 'it was a job that needed two people'. But Second Employee said she was 'having a meeting with a man from the Council about the office lease' - I don't know what this is a euphemism for, Larry - but that he should let me out immediately because 'Ghost cannot be trammelled'. Well, First Employee came off the phone, Larry, and let me out straight away: but it was too late. The car, and my wonderful calm grey future, were receding into the distance!

Esso says, well they can't have wanted you that much, Ghost, if they wouldn't wait more than ten minutes: but, frankly, this Commitment to Efficiency impresses me even more. Larry, could you please contact the wonderful new bungalow and explain to my new Employee that I was Seized, Kidnapped and Prodded, and that afterwards First Employee Faffed and Delayed Things, and if she could send the car again on Thursday when both the Employees are out then this time I will be ready.

Also, Larry, Second Employee gave Permission to Second Employee's Brother and His Partner to visit with their Large Leggy Hairy-Eared Companion, who we understand identifies as a Dog. Anyway, he Encountered Esso on his way out to the garden, and Esso Fluffed Himself Up, and Second Employee's Brother's Partner stated for the record that she *personally* considered Sid the Dog to have been 'shit scared'.

Esso and I also heard Second Employee's Mother, Larry, describing a programme she had seen on the television which suggested that twenty different types of bacteria can be transferred during a cat bite, *every individual one of which* is deadly. I do not wish to encourage Esso in his persecution complex, Larry, but it was clearly a pointed statement. Esso says he is absolutely tired of his reputation as a massive scary scrapper with TEETH when actually he is sensitive and artistic. He says, do you know he is currently reading Baudrillard to form an opinion on how Baudrillard would respond to the current political climate. It is my advice, Larry, take it or leave it, that you do not engage with Esso about Baudrillard, because it merely encourages him, and I for one have heard quite enough.

As you can see, Larry, it has been a challenging week: the only positives are that I no longer have toothache and can eat my BISCUITS with increased alacrity, and that now I know Second Employee has managed to learn one thing during her tenure, which is that I Cannot Be Trammelled. Who knew she was capable! Anyway, Larry, it is all academic now, as on Thursday I shall be off to my new Ammonite Home - if you can confirm the time for the car, I will be there, and this time *nothing can possibly go wrong!*

**June 2024**

Larry, this is Esso, Ambassador to the High Peak and Minister for Aesthetic Standards. Larry, I am notifying you that I have had to take Decisive Action. I'm sorry if this causes you a diplomatic issue or additional work, but I really feel I had no choice. It is my understanding, Larry, that under constant Pressure and Whining from Ghost you had organised a transfer for her to 'a very rigid woman in linen who lives in a Grey-Painted Bungalow in the Derbyshire Dales and there is no crochet or wool or cobalt blue paint or silliness or anything and everyone just sits upright on wooden chairs and lives the life of the mind'. This is how this has been represented to me, by Ghost, finally, at three o'clock this morning, when she came to wake me up and tell me for the fourth time that she did not love Second Employee *one little bit* and was not going to miss her at *all*.

Well, at that point, Larry, I said, Ghost, you have now woken me up four times to tell me this and frankly I am starting to think you are protesting too much, what is really going on. And then, Larry, I got the full story, and how the car was coming to pick

Ghost up today and she was going to have a wonderful new life and she didn't need anyone to stroke her and tell her she was the softest cat in the High Peak anyway, because, and I quote, 'familial affection is bourgeois'.

Larry: this Will Not Do. This is an action Ghost would have regretted. I told her this, and she said, well, Esso, it is too late to change things now: but she had a sad look in her yellow eyes (we don't get those eyes from Granny On Our Mother's Side and there *is* no House Demon heritage, despite what Chunky Black Cat might have been saying at the last meeting of the North Buxton Monochrome Cat Alliance). So I said to her, well, Ghost, I am afraid I am vetoing this Nonsense, and if you insist on going through with it, then I have two photos which may find themselves leaked to the Press: so I shall leave you to consider that very seriously. I showed them to her. She said, Esso, I believe you to be a literal monster: but, Larry, secretly, I think she was relieved. I have turned the car away. Ghost is asleep (or pretending to be asleep) on the sofa. The Employees must never know, or they would worry. I shall leave everything to settle just for today: and then, tomorrow, I think finally we will really be in a position to properly concentrate on delivering the Strategic Plan!

[Note from Esso: the photos involved Ghost, that purported handicraft-hater, curled up fast asleep on crochet and on patchwork. I just wish Ghost could accept this side of herself: but maybe she will get there one day.]

**June 2024**

Larry and the Catinet, this is Ghost, Ambassador to the High Peak and Minister for Aesthetic Standards which I am having to work exceptionally hard to maintain at the moment. The Employees are having a Very Silly Party next month to celebrate both of them having Big Birthdays this year and also having been married for Seven Years, which is the Seven Year Itch, so they are getting the party in quickly in case they have to get divorced straight afterwards.

I have said to Esso, if they do get divorced, I personally will have to go with Second Employee because she is the one who needs more Supervision and I think First Employee is capable of Porting A Mortgage and understanding how to pay a gas bill. So that is all sorted. Well, Esso says, no Ghost I am going with Second Employee as well because I love her and I am her Special Precious Velvety Esso; but that is all nonsense and I will not listen to him when the time comes. Which it will. Mark my words.

Anyway, the Employees have got to stay together at least long enough to have their Party, and they are trying to make the Embassy look DECENT and as if capable people live in it who have not given up in the face of continual rain and all those stairs. So Second Employee is wandering about with a Paint Brush and a Check List, and First Employee is organising Julian the Handyman to come and Fix various Issues outside. I am Very Fed Up: because Julian has Opinions on everything, and especially my aesthetic value as a small white cat with Discrete Black Patches, which I am having to listen to; and every time I see Second Employee carefully improving the Cutting In of the Orange Paint in the Dining Room I think, this is all Wasted Effort and what she should be doing is painting it Ammonite. In fact I think I might try to take Julian to one side and say to him, look, do not bother with your washing of the Outside PVC on the porch with your Pressure Washer, let us wait until the Employees go out and get this sorted properly: I will go and get a batch of Johnstone's Covaplus Vinyl Matt appropriately colour matched from the shop at the bottom of the road and we will Crack On. Esso says, look, Ghost, don't get involved: let the Employees get on with it, do not give yourself extra work. And there is some truth in that, because although the weather is TERRIBLE at the moment there are still Opportunities for Sunny Patches and I think I may just spend a few weeks lying in them, regrouping, and trying to get some rest for once!

**July 2024**

Larry, this is Esso, Ambassador to the High Peak and Minister for Aesthetic Standards, with a Helpful Reminder for the Catinet

- although firstly, Larry, may I congratulate you on having successfully made another new appointment, although I do sympathise with what you were saying on the Zoom social last week about none of them ever lasting very long. You really have had a surprising number of Employees!

[Note from Esso: this one was called Keir, I believe, which is a very similar name to the one First Employee has, who is called Keith. Our particular Keith modelled himself when young on other Keiths, for example Keith Moon and Keith Richards, although I understand he was a 'bit livelier'. I do not know if Larry's Keir modelled himself on other Keirs, or indeed if there were any. Second Employee's Ape Name is Susie, and *apparently* her EX told her it was 'only a suitable name for a stripper or a poodle!'. Imagine! And that is what I know about Employee Names.]

Anyway, well done on a successful process at least! Ghost says she can't believe she never thought of just getting our own Employees voted out, but luckily I caught her before she started leafleting Graham next door, although I understand she's already booked the Shop Down The Road for a day in August as a polling station. So that's yet one more thing I shall have to finesse. They won't want to be setting up a polling booth and having to move the sausage cabinet.

Anyway, I thought we should remind the Catinet that, although sometimes our Employees make Interesting Suggestions, we of course don't have to act on them. Because we know better. So for example, earlier I found myself resplendent on the Downstairs Sofa: Second Employee had just washed all the loose covers and dried them, which I understand is quite a feat without a tumble dryer and when it has apparently 'rained every single day since the beginning of last September'. As a consequence, she made the suggestion that I perhaps not sit on it for a while 'with my wet feet and wet black fur that gets everywhere like tumbleweed crossed with velcro'. It was an interesting suggestion, and I did, of course, take her point: but I decided to overrule her, because although there may well be 'at least 93 other places you can sit to dry yourself off just for a few days until the rain stops, Esso', the Downstairs Sofa is *currently* my favourite.

Similarly, the other day she suggested I not 'put my big furry bum' on the crochet she was in the middle of doing: but, of course, I like to get up close and personal with crochet and infuse it with my Feline Energies, so unfortunately I was forced to overrule her again. Of course, she doesn't mind, because I am a Kind and Benevolent Employer; and also, Second Employee's Annual Appraisal is coming up so she isn't rocking the boat. Ghost says she has found 'a round crochet horror on the second floor' and as a consequence wants to 'feed in very robustly to the appraisal process': but, Larry, I am still a bit cross with Ghost for causing all that trouble about the grey bungalow in Derbyshire Dales, so I've told her for the moment just to concentrate on delivering the Strategic Plan!

## July 2024

Larry, this is Ghost, Ambassador to the High Peak - Larry, for God's sake can you quash the rumours that are circulating AGAIN about me never having been off Second Employee's Ridiculous Throw since she finished it, and, WORSE, that I share it with Esso! I most certainly do not! Thank you, Larry, I'm just in the middle of the annual Employee Appraisal process over here but when it's finished I'll be in touch with a very hard-hitting REPORT!

## July 2024

Larry. This is Ghost, *Actual* Minister for Aesthetic Standards, and Ambassador to the High Peak, with a particularly hard-hitting report: about the credulity of Esso, the sneakiness of Employees, and a possible PLOT involving the stallholders of the Buxton Octagon Antiques Fair.

Larry, I am so frustrated. I performed Second Employee's Appraisal a few weeks ago, and I really felt that whatever I did I could not get her to pass; which was obviously very difficult because, as you know, if she fails her appraisal then I would have to just put her on the train and suggest to her that she starts a new life wherever the train goes to, possibly Levenshulme. And of course that would be terrible, particularly for Levenshulme. Anyway, Esso caught me just as I was officially writing her score in her performance record in the Strategic Plan, and honestly, Larry, he HAGGLED and CARPED and QUERIED and said who was going to stroke his ears and tell him he was The Best Cat (which he certainly is not) if I got rid of Second Employee, and so eventually I agreed to mark her as Borderline Unacceptable rather than Definitely Unacceptable and allow her to stay. Larry, even as I wrote her score officially in the Plan I knew it was a mistake. Well, I was ONCE AGAIN proved correct, because this weekend the Employees did two terrible, terrible things.

Firstly, the Employees had their Silly Party, for which they invited a lot of Disreputable People to come to the Embassy. Larry, every time I think we have finally Bottomed Out and Got A Handle on Second Employee's Family and that there cannot possibly be any more people to come and look at Esso and say, look Susie, is this the one who bit your father, she produces some more. What made it worse, Larry, is that Second Employee's Mother kept running TOURS of the Embassy to show people, and so Disreputables kept Popping Up to the Top Floor where I was on my beanbag, saying, look, there is another cat here, isn't it pretty. I have made my feelings clear about the matter to Second Employee, and I am exceptionally CROSS that because Esso made me let her pass her appraisal it makes it more difficult for me to get rid of her on performance grounds until the next one.

Difficult: but not impossible.

[Note from Ghost: interestingly, at this particular gathering, we managed to solve the issue of How To Wrangle Family In Wheelchairs when they are attending a gathering on multiple floors and are always *quite determined* to be on whatever floor they are not on at that particular moment. It turned out, rather unbelievably, that Second Employee has yet ANOTHER cousin, who is a Competitive Weightlifter: and he was able to pick up Aunty Kath and her wheelchair *in their joint entirety,* and carry them down into the basement and out into the garden where all the Gossip was going on, so she could be appropriately involved. Aunty Kath only protested once, rather weakly, when she demanded to be placed down in the porch so she could process what had just happened, and have a Panic Attack in comfort: but Second Employee told her firmly that was Not An Option, as the Porch is a strategic point which blocks the back door, and it meant if Aunty Kath was there panicking then no-one could get past to replenish the Sausages. This is something I have myself found (the strategy, not the sausages). This is why I pee in it so frequently and energetically. In fact, I feel that managing to think in this strategic way is one of the few things I have ever noticed which are to Second Employee's Credit.]

Finally, Larry, something else has happened, which I really consider unforgivable. The Employees wandered off today to look at the Buxton Octagon Antiques and Collectables Fair. I encourage this as an interest, Larry. I understand there is more than one Catinet Employee who enjoys collecting small ceramic representations of Employers, and I think, of all the ridiculous things Employees can do, that is one of the more wholesome and harmless. I also understand that Second Employee likes to look at things carefully and say, hmm, Clarice Cliff; and, so long as she *only looks*, I *personally* feel no harm can come from that. Anyway, we waved them off, and at that point Esso said, is this the same Antiques fair that Second Employee got the gold Foo Dogs from? Well, Larry, I went cold. How could I have forgotten? But then I thought, she is hardly likely to do it again. How many ridiculously large Foo Dogs can there possibly be in Buxton? So imagine my HORROR when she came back with another! An even bigger one! It is honestly unbelievable. She 'had to buy him because he had lost his friend somewhere around 1983'.

Well. Well. It is clear to me, Larry, that what has happened is that the Buxton Antiques and Collectables Fair Stallholders have Got Together and decided that FINALLY they have found a sucker who will take their Ridiculous Foo Dogs off their hands, so they will keep bringing them to the Fair in ever-increasing quantities and sizes, and Second Employee will keep bringing them home in Triumph and putting them in Silly Places. I imagine people are RIFLING through storage units all around Derbyshire even as I write, shouting, Thank God, at last I can get rid of all those bloody Foo Dogs, taking up all this room and nobody has bought *a single one* since I got rid of two pairs to that macrobiotic restaurant in 1976!

Well, I have pondered deeply and without prejudice on all these things, Larry, and I have come to one, inescapable conclusion. I imagine you have come to the same conclusion by now. Yes: that I should not be expected to face these tribulations alone, or, only with Esso, who is Not Impartial. So, I have WhatsApped Alejandro, the Goat Spokesman. I have said, Alejandro, it is time for you to stop Finding Yourself. I want you to put down your Hot Yoga Mat, Wave Goodbye to Hebden Bridge, and bring the Goats to Buxton. I need help. I need reinforcements. I need someone to deal with the Foo Dogs, Second Employee, Second Employee's Family and, in particular, Second Employee's Mother! I have received a Heart reaction on my WhatsApp, Larry, and it informs me that Alejandro is typing. It can take a while - hooves - but I am confident that, by my next report, I will have an Active Iberian Goat Militia in operation in Buxton, the Foo Dogs and Second Employee's Mother will be subdued, and Order Will Be Supreme once more!

**August 2024**

Larry, this is Esso, Ambassador to the High Peak and Minister for Aesthetic Standards. Larry, please imagine me looking STERN; because I have Serious Things to report today. First, however, I would like to remind the Catinet that, when they take on an Employee, that Employee almost becomes a member of the family. We cannot get rid of them or rehome them just because they become old and difficult, or because we want to get a dog, or move somewhere where Employees are impractical. I know Employees can be a lot of trouble - believe me, I do know that, especially after this week - but when we have made a commitment to give a home to an Employee we cannot renege on it, no matter how utterly exhausting they are. I have been explaining this to Ghost, because unfortunately, Second Employee has been DISCOVERED to have done a number of challenging things this week.

Firstly, Larry, it turns out that she believes she has Taught Herself Spanish on Duolingo, even though I really don't think she has got any proper understanding of Usted and has also decided 'not to bother with the accents because they are a lot of trouble and no-one really cares anyway'. Luckily Ghost discovered this just before the Iberian Goat Militia descended on their bikes: because, as she says, the last thing we need is Second Employee practicing her Imperatives on Alejandro: but it means we have had to put them all up in the Palace Hotel pending a Proper Plan, and they are all Making Hay again in the In-House Restaurant. I'm very sorry, Larry, but my expenses claim this month is going to be considerably larger until I can explain to Alejandro we can't have Goats ordering Cocktails and Tunnocks Teacakes on Deliveroo at all hours of the day and night. Alejandro really loves Tunnocks Teacakes. I suppose you don't get them in Andalucia. But don't worry, Ghost is working on how to say it in Spanish *as I write*. I suggested we ask Second Employee, but Ghost said, you can stick that suggestion right up your bum sideways, Esso, so I did not press the matter.

Then, secondly, Larry, Ghost had a Suspicion: and she was right. It turns out, Larry, that the Employees have owned the Small Flat Next Door for a while: and, now the Sitting Tenant has moved on, they are renovating it. Which is fine: except, in a display of Consummate Tactlessness, Second Employee has decided to paint the whole thing in Dulux Trade Pure Brilliant White, and has been telling Ghost how 'nice and bright' it has made the flat, and how she had 'decided to keep it neutral because she doesn't want to impose her taste on a new tenant'. Ghost told me, Larry, that when Second Employee said this to her, she 'literally nearly dropped down dead right in the Dahlias from the garden centre in Peak Village at the ASTONISHING HYPOCRISY', and in fact she only did not because Chunky Half-Tail Black Cat was watching and 'she would not give him the satisfaction'. I have to be honest: it is not ideal. People keep looking in the flat and exclaiming at How Much Brighter it is, and Second Employee is wandering about with her paintbrush, even though Interim Summer Employee and Second Employee's Cousin (another one, Larry) have done most of the work, looking very pleased with herself; and, as far as I can see, not applying what she has learned about the Desirability Of White Paint to the Embassy at all. It is all very difficult.

What is even more difficult, Larry, is that the Employees wandered off to a Wedding on Wednesday, at which it was Critically Important that Everyone, Especially Second Employee Who Has Form, Looked Normal And *Not Odd*: and it turns out that, despite having said all week that she would 'just have a good rub down at the last minute with some white spirit', Second Employee was not, after all, able to get all the Dulux Trade Satinwood off the bits of her that had not been covered by her Dungarees, and so had to go to the festivities looking A Little Eccentric. She did suggest, Larry, that as her hands were the worst, perhaps she could find some gloves: but the last thing I needed *in the world* was Second Employee wandering round Southwark looking as if she was trying to channel Madonna circa 1985: so I had to veto this, and now a solution must be found to the fact that Second Employee is in wedding photographs, alongside normal people who are wearing clothes from purchased from shops or reputable internet vendors, clad in patchwork, grinning, and covered in paint.

I do not know what the solution is: I cannot always be the ideas cat. Perhaps we could find the photographer and steal their camera and stamp up and down on it. I do not know if this will work in these days of Digitisation. So I will pass this one back to you, Larry, as Southwark is more your manor than mine, but of course if you ever need anything 'finessing' up here (even as far as Whaley Bridge), I am ready and willing.

So, as you can see, it has been a Trying Week: and we are just resting as much as we can before the Challenges Of The Next. Oh, before I sign off, Ghost gave me a cryptic message to pass on and has refused to expand: she said to tell you that, can you ignore the rumour about her and the Owl which is circulating, and can you confirm the conversation you apparently both had in 2020 at which you confirmed that gravity didn't apply to her and she didn't need to worry. I do not know what she means, Larry: but I shall assume it is nothing for anyone to be concerned about!

[Note from Esso: I discovered subsequently that Ghost had sent Second Employee into a PANIC by hearing an owl hooting outside the open bedroom window as the Employees were going to bed, and setting off through the window, which is three floors up and has a Concrete Patio underneath, after it. It is my understanding that Second Employee had to WRESTLE her back in, then put her out of the room, and shut the door. It is my further understanding that Second Employee opened her eyes in the half-light of dawn to see Ghost, having gained entry to the bedroom by emotionally manipulating First Employee on one of his many prostate-related toilet trips, sitting on the the open window frame, leaning out of it casually, and staring straight at her. Second Employee jumped up, half asleep, to grab at Ghost: who stepped elegantly back down, fixed her with a look, and walked out of the room, pointedly; underlining *once more* the fact that she will Not Be Trammelled.]

# Chapter 9
# Autumn 2024: A Beanbag Fulfils its Destiny

**September 2024**

Larry, this is Ghost, Ambassador to the High Peak and Minister for Aesthetic Standards. Larry, I just need to update you with a few things. Firstly I have moved into the Silly Flat Next Door which the Employees think they are renting out. I am using it as a Meditation Space when I CANNOT BEAR the Embassy any longer. Esso says this will not work because there is a tenant moving in at the end of the month, but he can move out again as far as I am concerned and move somewhere else. So that is that, because I really think I need some RESPITE from having to live somewhere where, for example, only today Second Employee wandered in with an enormous framed jigsaw featuring a woman in a gold headdress with two lionesses stating that she 'couldn't believe she got it from Oxfam for only £1.99'. Nor could Esso or I, Larry, and nor, I imagine, could the Oxfam staff, who had probably already been arguing amongst themselves about who was going to wrestle the ridiculous thing into their HATCHBACK and take it to the tip at Waterswallows.

Secondly, I have temporarily installed the Goats at Thornbridge Hall down the road. I had the idea when the Employees went there for Lunch and remarked that there were 'ducks and a goat now and all sorts'. I felt that if there was one goat there could be more goats, perhaps twenty more Spanish goats, and so did Alejandro: then we googled, and we felt that Hall Owners who had the attitude that they had already demonstrated towards the Red Tape of the Peak DIstrict Planning Authority were the type of people who could cope with an Unexpected Goat Militia.

So the Goats are all installed there quite happily, and it is working very well; because, while they are on the spot for when I launch my Offensive Against Second Employee's Brother, Thornbridge Hall is now paying for their Tunnocks Teacake Deliveries. Could you just mention it to them, Larry: I really haven't had the time yet.

Alejandro also tells me he has found a fabulous shop in Bakewell called Brocklehursts, where he is going to buy his red trousers and a quilted gilet; but I have told him he is here to destabilise the class system not prop it up, so we are still in discussion about that - he says he can perhaps see himself being a proto-Anarcho-Syndicalist in the vein of the Diggers, but he will have to see what trousers they wear first 'because not everything looks right on his legs.'

Thirdly, Larry, Esso says to tell you that the Rumours that his teeth recently bit Second Employee's Brother are untrue. Well I have told you as instructed but obviously he is talking nonsense, we all saw Esso chomping right down on Second Employee's Brother and it is a good job he does not Bear Grudges, however much I might disapprove of his ridiculous hyper-realistic sausage rolls. It is also a good job Second Employee's Mother was herself chomping down on some Millionaire's Shortbread at the time and missed it, because otherwise none of us would ever have heard the end of it.

I understand, Larry, that Second Employee's Mother has been sent a Leaflet detailing the clubs and activities she may wish to attend in her capacity as Carer for Second Employee's Father, and that the one she is interested in is a Sailing Club. Can I just notify you that there are few things I feel would be more unhelpful for the country at this juncture than Second Employee's Mother in charge of a small Catamaran. Esso says, look Ghost, they wouldn't let her do that straight away, they would start her off small: but Larry, even the thought of Second Employee's Mother perhaps haring across Ladybower Reservoir on a motorised paddle board is anathema to me. Could you please notify whoever organises this nonsense that Carers should only ever be encouraged to do quiet things which don't cause trouble: possibly jigsaws, although obviously not large gold ones of women and lions, as these might fall into the wrong hands.

Really, Larry, the difficulties I have to Anticipate and Prevent: but don't worry, Esso is updating the Risk Register again, and we are already beginning to plan for the delivery of the High Peak Embassy Strategic Plan 24/25 3rd Quarter!

**September 2024**

Larry, this is Esso, Ambassador to the High Peak and Minister for Aesthetic Standards. Larry, something very interesting has happened! Second Employee has purchased a rather marvellous Beanbag Footstool, which arrived in a DHL van. Second Employee had consulted the Tracking on the Website and was expecting it: so when a DHL van pulled up she went out and said to the driver, who was an unobjectionable young man, have you got my parcel. The young man consulted his list and said, no, I have not: but Second Employee was not convinced, and watched him BEADILY as he delivered something to the man in the flat next door: and even more BEADILY as he looked at her nervously and said, no, I definitely haven't got anything for you, I have checked, and got in the van and drove off. Second Employee then checked her TRACKING again, which did not tell her anything useful, but had a profile of the young man who had denied knowledge of her beanbag, which informed her that his favourite song was Don't Look

Back In Anger, by Oasis. At this point Second Employee was looking forward in anger, out of the front window onto the A6: but then she saw the DHL van drive back and pull up outside the house again, and the young man get out and shamefacedly give her a parcel because his 'system had been being difficult and had only just told him now'.

Second Employee says she was Gracious in the Victory of having been proved Entirely Correct: and we are delighted with the beanbag. It is a good size, made of navy blue corduroy and stuffed with beanbag filling, which makes it very comfortable for Ambassadors. It is really like sleeping on air. Second Employee says that years ago she made a beanbag out of patchwork and filled it herself with polyester pellets and a jug: and she says that when she had finished she was entirely coated with polyester pellets and looked like a Yeti, and she was still finding them until the day she fled from that house with only the Small Blue Punto, some leopardskin poledancing shorts, and a pack of Tarot cards. The patchwork beanbag now lives on the top landing, and Ghost loves it very much. Second Employee says she is not losing another beanbag to cats and that this one is for her, to put her feet on. I would not dream of commandeering Second Employee's Footstool Beanbag, Larry, and I resent the implication, but I understand sometimes things have Difficult Associations for her and that can cause her to be slightly more Tactless than normal. Anyway, the beanbag is for

Second Employee, and I am sure she will get lots of use out of it and enjoy it very much!

## September 2024

Larry, this is Ghost, Very Important Top Ambassador to the High Peak and Minister for Aesthetic Standards. Larry, I have been trying to do my update for DAYS, but Second Employee has been FAFFING ABOUT. She said, Ghost, it is all difficult at the moment, Dad has been diagnosed with Alzheimers and we are all frazzled, no matter how much you follow me step for step squeaking loudly everywhere I go you will just have to wait a little bit. Well, Larry, I cannot wait and I shouldn't be expected to. I am very annoyed. However, as a Caring Employer, I have agreed just this once to only do a short UPDATE, even though an enormous number of ridiculous things have happened; but I shall be making an extensive note of this on Second Employee's record.

Just as an aside, Larry, Esso says can you check that, whatever or *whoever* Alzheimer's is, it is not caused by the teeth of cats acting independently: and can you make sure we have that in writing just in case anyone {*cough* Second Employee's Mother *cough*} ever has a burst of energy and spends it on being litigious. Can I also add to that, Larry, that I think it would be good to document that the teeth which act independently are the ones which belong to Esso and not me. *Mine* are under control. Thank you. Good. That is now sorted.

Anyway, Larry, Second Employee has started another Silly Crochet Item. I was just about to deploy CLAWS when I was distracted with the absolutely terrible news that Second Employee's Brother is going to be on the Local News with his Very Silly Hyperrealist Paintings Of Inappropriate Items. Larry, there is no good way of spinning this: I consider it a PR disaster of epic proportions, and can I advise all members of the Catinet to make sure their Employees aren't watching Look North on either Friday or Monday coming because we aren't sure which day it is going to be on. My only comfort, Larry, is that Second Employee generally goes by her married surname because she 'just got to a point where she couldn't face spelling her name on the phone one more time', and so it will be difficult for anyone to link them and it may still be possible to keep it a secret. I will do all I can. I will confess, I was hoping the Iberian Goat Militia would be a little more help: but after they saw an extremely unfortunate Facebook post recently they are busy working on their first album, which I understand involves covers of Prog Rock classics reinterpreted for ukulele.

[Note from Ghost: this is an example of where we should not allow Employees, or indeed Goats, to have Facebook. It was very unfortunate that Alejandro was reading over my shoulder when someone suggested Prog Rock as a suitable Goat interest: he was straight down to Argos for a ukulele. I really wish Employees would consider what the consequences might be as they are typing away, because the Goats, as they say, ran with it, and are currently working on their second album, a Captain Beefheart tribute, a cover album of Trout Mask Replica: and really if I have to listen to the rehearsals one more time I might become quite restive. However much I enjoy Alejandro's canapés. Which, to be fair, do compensate for a lot: but not for Captain Beefheart. So please consider this when you are typing your ill-judged words, Employees.]

Esso has heard the demo, and he says it is 'an acquired taste'. As I'm sure you can appreciate, Larry: this is not ideal. In fact, I will go further: I have consulted the Strategic Plan: we are not where we need to be right now. We must face this. I am about to undertake a Radical Rewrite of the Whole Plan, Larry, and I will be back in touch the *very minute* I have a Solution!

**October 2024**

Larry, this is Esso, Ambassador to the High Peak and Minister for Aesthetic Standards: Larry, another letter!

'To Mister S.O. Puss Puss cat agen,

Yore Siouxie [I am not sure why they had decided to trial this interesting spelling of Second Employee's name, especially after their triumph last time. As you can imagine, it is not the correct one. At least, I'm not aware that it is. Let's hope it isn't. Esso] haz been SEEN going too the flee mRket.

Duz Gost no she duz this? Gost wud bee mad. Bee kerrful we do not tell Gost.

Yores

The Chesterfield JinJer Cats Allianse.

Honestly, Larry, I really am having trouble working out the motivation here. Is it a threat to tell Ghost? Are they fans of Ghost? Does her reputation precede her? In any case, I do not want them going telling her Second Employee is going walking round flea markets. I do not think it would be helpful. If Second Employee starts bringing home all sorts of things from flea markets then that might be a different issue: but in the meantime we cannot keep her under constant surveillance, and frankly I personally feel the Chesterfield Ginger Cats' Alliance should turn their minds to things more cerebral!

Also, Larry, just to notify you that I decided it wasn't good for Second Employee to have a Footstool Beanbag: as Ghost says, we need to encourage her to get off her Bum and move as much as possible. It would be terribly sad for it to go to waste, so it is very lucky that it really is the perfect size and shape for a larger Ambassador to lie on his back on, with his legs in the air at interesting angles. We're all delighted with this solution, Larry, because Second Employee hates waste just as much as the rest of us!

**October 2024**

Larry, this is Ghost, Ambassador to the High Peak and Minister for Aesthetic Standards, just to let you have my and Esso's new publicity photos for you to put on file in case we need something to illustrate how PROFESSIONAL and HARDWORKING members of the Diplomatic Service are. I selected them very carefully. As you can see, we are both represented in Characteristic Poses: me, alert and ready to take on any challenge: Esso, fast asleep on the rug with his legs in the air. I really feel they illustrate our respective characters. You might want to use one of them, perhaps, for an article in the Financial Times or an extended opinion piece in the Spectator. I can't imagine which one you will choose.

By the way, Esso says he is undertaking an Extended Rewrite of the Yoga Mat Protocol: he says we need to specify that as soon as the mat comes out he needs to be notified so he can 'run over chirruping and get right down there with Second Employee to help her with her alignment': but, I happen to know that Second Employee isn't entirely on board, because she was apparently 'trying to do a side plank this evening' when Esso 'ran over, purred, stuck his bum in her face, headbutted her ear, bit her wrist and now she has got a crick in her neck and she has got to drive to Chesterfield tomorrow'. Well, I personally am amazed that she has kept up the fiction of 'driving to Chesterfield' for almost three quarters of a year when anyone sensible knows she only gets as far as Morrisons, but, that besides, I do not want disagreement over the Yoga Mat Protocol. It will be nothing but trouble. I am going to persuade Esso just to let it lie for the moment until Second Employee is over her cricked neck and has forgotten; and in the meantime I am getting on with my Strategic Plan rewrite, and, let me assure you, when I am done, things are going to be far more efficient around here!

**October 2024**

Larry, this is Ghost, Ambassador to the High Peak and Minister for Aesthetic Standards - Larry, I am so FRUSTRATED and EMBARRASSED by what the Employees have done recently that I really feel like perhaps entering a convent and spending my days from now on in quiet contemplation. Firstly, Larry, despite it all going Exceptionally Badly when we last allowed the Employees out to Spain - culminating in them eventually wandering back after a number of weeks with an enormous pot on Second Employee's arm and a Lot Of Nonsense Items including two Very Silly Moroccan Light Fixtures to which I am *still* not reconciled - Esso and I discussed it and agreed - well,

Esso persuaded me - that it would be safe to let them go again, although only for a week this time. What can go wrong, Ghost, he said. Well, Larry: he *did not tell me* when Second Employee WhatsApped him half way through to tell him that she had 'gone a bit mad with the ceramics on Torrox market' and 'was a bit worried about how she was going to get them back in her hand luggage now that Easyjet were so strict'. If he had DISCLOSED this communication appropriately as per Appendix 3M of the Strategic Plan, Larry, I would have Taken Over The Situation and I would have ensured that Second Employee, above all, did NOT BRING ANY OF HER NONSENSE BACK.

I note that First Employee, who has a sensible small rigid wheelie case rather than a rucksack with parrots on it, does not decide halfway through the holiday that there will definitely be a way of stuffing in it 'a small ironic bull with an interesting glaze and a carved tealight lantern in the shape of a pomegranate'. Because there clearly is not. But Esso did not respond sensibly. Instead he advised her - and, Larry, you won't believe this - to wear her dungarees on the plane and to stick anything she couldn't get in her bag in the front pocket. Where do you think an action like this would lead, Larry? I shall tell you: it led to Second Employee being Patted Down because the buckles on her Dungarees set off the scanner. It led to her Packing Out Her Front Pocket like a Kangaroo in order to get through boarding, where a very fierce Easyjet woman was striding up and down, shouting to people whose bags were Questionable Sizes, I Very

Much Hope You People are Speedy Boarding and Cabin Bag otherwise I shall have to take your bag and Put It In The Hold. Second Employee says she was on Pins the entire time because as well as the bull and the pomegranate she had some 'rather nice demi tasses and a splatter pattern jug' and she didn't want them being thrown around the hold, but luckily thanks to judicious Packing of Dungaree Pockets and nervous shuffling she got through, and actually she has found that the front pocket of dungarees is an excellent place for Books which otherwise take up a lot of room in bags. When I heard this, I went cold. Esso tried to hide it from me, but eventually he confessed. Yes, Larry: the book that Second Employee had in her dungaree pocket, title visible to all, was called Overcoming Perfectionism. I declare this, Larry, the day that Irony Died, and I am entirely unsure what Perfectionism Second Employee needs to worry about given that she has not *actually* done anything correctly since 1992.

Anyway, the Employees are back, now, Larry, although I have a couple of things to flag up. Firstly, I understand that Second Employee has just had her Fiftieth Birthday, which really is an almost unimaginable age. I do not know the usual lifespan of Employees, but it is probably generally only fifty years and six months, so obviously that is now something we need to put on the Risk Register and throw into the mix for future planning and Ammonite Bungalow Purposes. In fact, the minute she turned fifty, Second Employee came down with Flu, which First

Employee initially diagnosed as Reluctance to Accept Being Fifty Disease; but which now appears to be something else as she is wandering about coughing. So it is likely she is winding down physically.

Esso says, look Ghost, First Employee is *quite a bit older than that* and he's still fine so you are being silly: but, Larry, of course there are always outliers. Esso has never had a proper understanding of statistics. Secondly, you can rest assured that I am now totally in control of the situation: since they came back, I have not let Second Employee out of my sight. I have followed her everywhere. I have SQUEAKED. I have STRETCHED. I have PURRED. I have NIBBLED. I have LICKED, in a vain attempt to Smarten Her Up A Bit. Esso says, look how much you've missed Second Employee, Ghost, I really find it heartwarming: but of course this is nonsense. I am merely re-establishing control, and then next week we will finally be in a position to really crack on with the Strategic Plan!

**November 2024**

Larry, this is Esso, Ambassador to the High Peak. I just want to notify you, Larry, that although Second Employee has just had a shower with a kind of soap that is Particularly Bitey, possibly involving something that is also found in Catnip, I do not know, my teeth are Entirely Under Control; and no-one need be worried even a little bit. Not even though she has a Particularly

Bitey Smell. There is no need to worry, delivery of the Strategic Plan continues apace, and tonight I am concentrating on the bit of it that specifies Testing Of Employee Resilience By Gentle Laying-On Of Teeth. I personally think I will be very successful. I do hope all the Catinet have a lovely evening!

## November 2024

Larry, this is Esso, Ambassador to the High Peak and Minister for Aesthetic Standards, in what is a Worrying Time... Larry, a number of concerning things have happened this week. I have realised that the Devil has taken up residence in our coffee machine: Graham Next Door has found Deer Droppings just outside Our Back Gate, and there is nothing in the Risk Register which gives any indication of what to do with a Recalcitrant Group Of Roaming Muntjacs: and Second Employee has spent all November's housekeeping budget on a Vintage Balinese Mask which 'will protect us all'. I cannot stress enough, Larry, that this is a Developing Situation. I am trying my best to manage, but if I need input from you I will WhatsApp you ASAP!

[Note from Esso: my sole criticism of Second Employee is that I never feel she properly understands the risks attached to the Devil living in our coffee machine. She strokes my ears and says, it's all ok Mr Esso, it's just grinding the beans, don't be scared: but I am not scared! I am monitoring a Very Real Risk!]

## November 2024

Larry, this is Ghost: Ambassador to the High Peak, Minister for Maintaining Aesthetic Standards in Almost Impossible Circumstances, and Admirable Example Of Feline Persistence.

Larry, I will be honest. This week I nearly gave up. Second Employee brought home something so ridiculous I can hardly bear to talk about it. She said, look, Ghost, it's a rather fabulous Balinese Barong Mask, what do you think. Can you imagine, Larry. I have said before, I do not know even one sensible reason why Second Employee has been given a credit card. Esso says that Employees have certain rights and one of them is access to money. Well, *why* do they, Larry? Who has decided that? I haven't! I think we should look at this again, particularly in relation to Employees like Second Employee who are not very bright and who are also Unhelpfully Drawn to Silly Things, Like Large Dim Magpies.

Anyway, the damage is done, and Second Employee hung the Silly Barong Mask above the Silly Dresser while I looked at her with my Paddington Stare; but she was impervious because she is DIM. So I already felt quite Furious, when something even worse happened.

Visitors came - yes, Larry, AGAIN we are ALREADY over the Number of Permitted Visitors for Employees 3rd quarter

2024/2025, as stated in the Strategic Plan Appendix G (Permitted number of visitors 3rd quarter 2024/2025 = 0); and one of them walked in the sitting room, saw one of the Ridiculous Hyperrealistic Fried Eggs which Second Employee's Brother Paints Misguidedly, and said, oh my God, it is one of the famous eggs, how did you manage to get one. And it turns out, Larry, that a *number* of Very Silly People follow Second Employee's Brother on Instagram to try to get the eggs; and it is apparently very difficult because Second Employee's Brother is WEAK and cannot paint twenty four hours a day because 'he needs to sleep sometimes'.

Needs to sleep! You see, Larry, I told you laziness runs in that family. Always lounging around. I personally am Ever Alert: although First Employee did say of Esso that Esso's problem is he really needs 25 hours' sleep a day which is technically difficult for cats to get, and Esso says he has never felt so understood by anyone.

Anyway, I shall state categorically right now that I Will Not Have Second Employee's Silly Brother becoming Recognised by Random People who shouldn't be in the Embassy to start with, and just in case he ever becomes famous I wish to put out a statement distancing Esso and I from the whole Silly Situation. I shall start drafting it now.

Then, Larry, the Waitrose Delivery Man this week was Exceptionally Taken with me. Obviously I am an Unusually Pretty Cat, but even given that, he was quite mesmerised; and I really would like to notify you that I consider this type of thing Impertinence. I know other members of the Catinet often have to deal with various Supermarket Delivery People: perhaps we could share experience with a view to developing a code of practice. It may be, for example, that Iceland Deliverers are generally more respectful, or that Tesco have a higher level of Professionalism. I do not know. Second Employee says she likes the Waitrose Delivery People because they all live locally and 'understand the local roads so they don't turn up traumatised'. It is my understanding they have instituted their own Buxton Emergency Kits of Grit and Shovel, which they keep in the back of their vans in case of Difficulties: well this is what they say it is for. It could also be used to kidnap unusually pretty cats and turn them into Furry Hats, for example. So I am not in the least mollified.

Anyway, as you can imagine, after my Difficult Week I really felt quite despairing. I looked at the Train Timetable From Buxton and I thought: there must be a grey bungalow in Levenshulme with a sensible person living in it, I shall go and find it. Esso said, Ghost, don't be silly, it's raining and look how comfortable you are on the bit of the landing which has a hot water pipe underneath it, don't cut your nose off to spite your face. Well, as you know, Larry, I care nothing for Comfort where Principles are involved: but I thought about things carefully and I decided to give things one last try. I had a chat with the Barong Mask: apparently his name is Barry, and we agreed a Truce, and he is going to Spread Good Vibes and protect me from being put in any Waitrose Vans and also from the under-plinth heater, which I am not scared of, but which makes my ears go back: and I have decided to pee on the Silly Egg Painting. I am having a few dry runs first so I can get the angle right: but when I have it I am completely confident I can dissolve oil paints. In fact I think I could dissolve something much stronger. So as you can see, in almost impossible circumstances I am persevering, and *despite everything*, the Strategic Plan will be delivered in the High Peak!

**November 2024**

Larry, this is Esso, Ambassador to the High Peak. Second Employee has sprained her foot running, so she has fashioned a crude footstool out of a sewing stool and a cushion because it is painful to put her foot on the floor. I really feel sad for Second Employee that she hasn't got a beautiful, comfortable, Beanbag Stool like I have! I've barely left it since last Thursday. What a shame Second Employee didn't plan ahead and make sure she had one too - it would be absolutely perfect to rest a sprained foot on. I can't imagine why she didn't buy a lovely spare Beanbag Footstool at the same time as buying one for me. You're supposed to keep sprained feet elevated, you know.

I think I really ought to add Review Of Footstool Provision to the Strategic Plan!

# Chapter 10
# Winter 2024-2025: The Employees are Snowed In

**December 2024**

Larry, this is Ghost, Ambassador to the High Peak and Minister for Aesthetic Standards. Larry, there is only one way to say this; Esso is being a Lazy Arse. I am very unhappy. There was a very minor incident with Mr Kitler from Near The Brook, and Esso got a Very Silly Injury on his Middle, and now we have to have Vets and Dreamies and Antibiotics Disguised in Tuna and Second Employee Handwringing, and all sorts of nonsense. And I KNOW Esso is absolutely fine now but still he's lounging about on the Downstairs Beanbag purring away while Second Employee strokes his ears and tells him he's a big brave boy. Which he *certainly isn't*! While I have to do all the work! Could you deal with this, please, Larry. I really think I should have a backdated pay rise for the last week, and possibly Esso needs a demotion for the moment... I definitely think I need some very serious support, because Christmas is coming up and the horrors wreaked in this Embassy in the name of festive decoration are already utterly indescribable! If things don't get better I'm going to have to tell the goats to put down their gilets and ukuleles and come here and sort things out!

**December 2024**

Larry, this is Ghost, Ambassador to the High Peak and Minister for Upholding Aesthetic Standards. Larry, I understand that we are supposed to be 'raising awareness of rescue animals' at the moment, and discussing how rewarding it is to give one a home. I have thought long and hard about this - I understand that the impulse behind it is genuine - but it isn't something I can support. In fact, I feel it's a little irresponsible. Rescues can have all sorts of Unhelpful Habits and Behavioural Difficulties which not everyone is able, or has the time, to deal with.

I allowed Esso to talk me into Adopting Rescue Employees during the time he and I were staying in our temporary accommodation which was Sue From Cats' Protection's Garage, deciding on our new career: but, knowing what I know now, if I am honest, I wouldn't do it again. I would go to a proper, licensed Employee Breeder, where I could make an informed judgment about temperament and IQ. I think members of the Catinet really need to think very carefully about what they want from Employees: Pointless Affection, or Efficient Strategic Plan Delivery. Obviously that question is rhetorical.

I hope Christmas Preparations are going well Chez Toi, Larry, and not being Derailed by Employees attending silly weddings, 'being tired', and then failing to produce Coconut Ice in a Timely Manner for Hampers!

## December 2024

Hello everyone, this is Esso, Ambassador to the High Peak. Ghostycat and I would like to wish everyone - even Employees - a Very Happy Christmas and a Productive New Year of Strategic Plan Delivery! We are not quite at our absolute Peak Of Efficiency here - Second Employee is lying on her back on the sofa, whimpering about Not Wanting To Bloody Wrap Everything, and First Employee seems to have inadvertently bought a turkey that will serve fifteen people - but I have every confidence that by tomorrow lunchtime it will all be a well-oiled machine! We hope you all have a lovely time, and we will see you on the other side!

## January 2025

Larry. This is Ghost, Ambassador to the High Peak and Minister for Aesthetic Standards, with an EXPOSÉ which will ROCK THE CATINET RIGHT TO THE CORE. Larry, I have been frustrated this weekend. I really felt we were not making the progress on the Strategic Plan January 25 that I had been expecting. First, we managed to lose the Employees after Christmas. Luckily,

Esso finally tracked them down to a Hotel in Huntingdon which was apparently a 'bit like Fawlty Towers although everyone had excellent intentions and the breakfasts were fabulous'; but it is not good for the Employees to be away getting Funny Ideas and then coming back looking as if they have been through a hedge backwards. Second Employee, in fact, looked as if she had been through a hedge backwards and then gone through it forwards again on purpose in preparation for going through it backwards a second time.

I really am going to have to deal with her this quarter. I have been LICKING very energetically but really there is only so much I can do without an extremely scissor-happy hairdresser, an eyebrow waxer and a Dyson airwrap at the very least: but I am reluctant to spend the Embassy budget when it should really all go on BISCUITS. So it is all very difficult.

I do not know what the Employees were doing while they were away, Larry, but I understand they were 'meeting people'. I believe one of the people to be First Employee's Silly Friend Who Works On AI, because whenever Second Employee has conversations about AI she always reacts in the most unhelpful way possible, i.e by Asserting The Value Of The Handmade, vowing to get an allotment, and getting out the particularly silly book about Making Your Own Shoes and wondering whether to make a start on creating her own moccasins. I do not know who else she was Meeting, but I would just advise the Catinet that Second Employee has not been given the appropriate clearance for Unaccompanied Discussions and so anyone conversing with her without me present is in direct contravention of the Strategic Plan Appendix D.

[Note from Ghost: I still suspect Second Employee of having met Other Employees, and I shall make her confess one of these days.]

Now to my EXPOSÉ. Because I was frustrated with our slow pace ref: Strategic Plan delivery, I said to Esso, look, Esso: here I am doggedly performing the daily Kitchen Inspection Protocol with particular attention to Sniffing Round The Back Of The Velvetiser, and yet you have spent almost seventy two hours on the beanbag with your legs in the air with only brief breaks for going to the toilet, sitting on Second Employee's Knitting, and drinking from the tap. What gives.

And he said to me, look, Ghost, I am actually the victim here: every time I try to get up to deliver on my workplan, I am Taken Over by the PURR and then I have no energy. It knocks me out. It exhausts me. There I am, desperately trying to get up and commence the Daily Sniffing Procedure and get a good start on the Weekly All-Borders Hissing Patrol but in reality I am felled and enervated by the PURR. It can come on at any time: it starts somewhere in my chest but when it spreads to my throat that is it. All my energy is gone, and all I can do is lie on my beanbag, PURRing away. Sometimes I muster all my resources and make a bold leap onto the rug and set off confidently to discuss important local matters with the rest of the North Buxton Monochrome Cat Alliance: but, oh no, the PURR starts again and I just have to flip over on the carpet with my LEGGIES all in the air, PURRing and PURRing. It really is terrible.

Well, Larry, I really felt for Esso and his struggle to deliver on his objectives against the PURR: in fact I have even heard First Employee remarking on it, saying, well Esso you had a good go there leaping off your beanbag, but actually you've not got any further than the rug, have you. Larry, Esso considers he has been very brave for a long time in his struggle against THE PURR, but now he is being open about his challenges. It is very difficult - even I am a victim of it sometimes! And I find it terribly poignant to think of all the members of the Catinet, throughout the world, trying to deliver on our Strategies without Succumbing to PURRing, Ennui, and Lassitude. It is actually *completely heroic*. So as well as delivering the Strategic Plan, Larry, and anticipating what Second Employee is going to do and stopping her, I shall now be raising awareness of this issue; and I will not rest until every cat is empowered to be the most efficient cat they can!

## January 2025

Larry, this is Esso, Ambassador to the High Peak. Larry, I really am struggling with the PURR tonight: whatever I do, it just keeps taking over! So Second Employee and I have agreed that we won't tell Ghost that I'm behind on my workplan and she's just eaten an enormous amount of fudge and we'll both get right back to delivering the Strategic Plan tomorrow!

## January 2025

Larry, this is Ghost, Ambassador to the High Peak and Minister for Aesthetic Standards. Larry, due to a Lack Of Forward Planning, the Employees were snowed in for a week and couldn't get out until this Tuesday. Esso says it was the happiest week of his life: he ENTIRELY succumbed to the PURR. The Employees pretended to be 'working from home'. Second Employee says she is 'writing a Strategic Plan' and she is 'going to get a Quality Mark'. The projection, Larry, is tragically poignant and also, of course, unbearably irritating: but, Larry, it does make me wonder - where is my Quality Mark? I should have at least THREE by now! Do you mind looking into it, while I try to ROUSE Esso to finally get him going on the Strategic Plan 2025, because, better late than never!

**January 2025**

Larry, This is Ghost, Ambassador to the High Peak, with a weekend reminder to Employees to get UP off their BUMS and start Strategic Plan delivery early! Don't be like Second Employee, who was WOEFULLY UNPREPARED for the Waitrose delivery and now can't remember where she has put her daffodils!

**January 2025**

Larry, this is a very, very worried Esso, Ambassador to the High Peak and Minister for Aesthetic Standards. Larry, First Employee has said a very, very worrying and terrible thing! Very terrible! A Letter Arrived, Larry, with details of our Special Ambassador Insurance. The rest of the Catinet may have something similar: it is a thing the Employees pay into every month which provides money if I or Ghost ever become Temporarily Indisposed. Well, First Employee read this Letter, because he is always very on top of things like that, and likes to put Monetary Amounts into his Budget Spreadsheet so he can say to Second Employee, Susie, we have got no money again this month so don't go buying wool, which Second Employee always studiously ignores. Anyway, in the letter, not only were Ghost and I described as 'breed: moggy', which really is terribly rude, and Ghost says we are both at least 75% house demon although that is not much better, but, it appears that my Insurance costs twice as much as Ghost's!

It is clear to me, Larry, that that is Blatant Sex Discrimination. And, as if that wasn't bad enough, First Employee said, well, that's it, Esso, we can't afford you any more. You'll have to go. You can stay until the current year runs out - Valentine's Day - but after that, sorry, you're out on your ear, you're just too expensive for us.

Larry! What a Thing to Say! Ghost says First Employee is 'obviously joking' because we 'have this every year when our insurance gets renewed' and I 'can't recognise irony', but, I *personally* do not think there is anything even remotely amusing about saying terrible, terrible things which imply the possible future separation of a Cat and his Beanbag. I will tell you what is *actually* funny: playing a lighthearted game involving separating a Sock from an Employee, as I did earlier. Second Employee and I had a really fabulous time! She said, Esso, you give me that sock back now because I've got to go out and I'm not at my best today to start with: but of course I didn't, I tapped her with my Clawsies and rolled round and round with the sock and we had *such* a lot of fun. I didn't let her have it for ages! So I will have no more 'irony' or 'obvious jokes' when I'm such a loved and valued member of this household, and First Employee can keep his Oppressive Budget Spreadsheet to himself!

## January 2025

Larry, this is Ghost, Ambassador to the High Peak and Minister for Aesthetic Standards - just to let the Catinet know that we've put the Employees on a Performance Improvement Plan, and we've begun by Observing Second Employee Very Closely over a twenty four hour period to see where we can make Efficiency Savings. Well, the short answer is, Everywhere - Second Employee wouldn't know Efficiency if she met it walking down Buxton High Street in a Dryrobe and a Woolly Hat - so I shall be collating our FINDINGS onto an Excel Spreadsheet and using them to make some VERY big changes round here in 2025!

## February 2025

Larry, this is Esso. Larry, I shall tell you what has annoyed me this week. Second Employee put a post on the Local Facebook Group asking if a Particular Black Cat who is always sitting on Next Door's Dustbin has a home, or if he needs to be ORGANISED by the local community and especially her. Well to start with I think Second Employee would be better off staying away from Local Facebook Groups, especially after the time she managed to have an argument with everyone in the vicinity about the provision *or lack of it* of Padel Courts in Buxton, when Second Employee is really no more likely to play Padel willingly than she is to skydive (and nor is anyone else in Buxton): but anyway she put this post on, and everyone said, oh, we all know that cat, he is such a lovely, friendly cat, and he is called Lokie The Cat, and he has a nice home. Well, that is fine. I mean, I don't know why Lokie didn't introduce himself formally to me and Ghost before now rather than just sitting on dustbins peering at people, but now we know who we are all dealing with and we can incorporate him properly into Strategic Plan Delivery.

But this is my question: why are there never any local facebook groups saying, *oh, we know Esso, he is a lovely cat, his fur is like velvet, his Strategic Plan delivery is almost faultless, and he really only bites people very rarely and they aren't all hospitalised, and, with the ones that are, no actual causal connection has ever really been proved*? Because there never are any local Facebook groups saying that. And I try not to be sad, but sometimes I think, I know the Employees love and appreciate me; and Ghost appreciates me to the extent that Ghost ever appreciates anything: but why aren't I More Generally Loveable? Is it my crooked tail? Is it my teeth? But then I pull myself together, because after all there are KPIs to be met, however sad one might feel, or however unappreciated one might be.

## February 2025

Larry, this is Ghost, Ambassador to the High Peak, UTTERLY DESPAIRING OF EMPLOYEES - I've just discovered Second

Employee eating a large blueberry muffin because she's 'been out to see a gym'. Not worked out in a gym or done anything useful in a gym - just looked at the gym to see if there was a SINGLE WEIGHT LIGHT ENOUGH FOR HER TO LIFT, and then walked home again. And now she's pleased with herself because if she joins it the walk home will be 'not only past Waitrose but past the nice cake shop as well'. Also, Larry, she says she really feels she's done well: because when she WhatsApped the man who ran the gym, his profile picture was of him Posing in a Thong: and she thought that when she went to meet him, it would go one of two ways: either he would be a Murderer, or he would want to tell her his thoughts on Creatine: and she was glad that neither of those things happened, and felt she had had an Excellent Escape.

Larry, we need a Proper Employee Health Drive in 2025 to improve efficiency, with Compulsory Runs And Cold Baths at Dawn and a diet SOLELY CONSISTING of protein bars and bran! No Effete Nonsense! Perhaps that will sort them out!

**February 2025**

Larry, this is Ghost, Ambassador to the High Peak, notifying you that I have Temporarily Suspended KPI monitoring and Strategic Plan delivery. Yes, Larry, you read that right. Second Employee's Father is very ill: I mean, I don't like to be cynical at a time like this, but I do think if people can't stand up to Esso's

Teeth, they'll be equally feeble standing up to Pneumonia and Sepsis. That is my opinion, and I imagine it will be borne out, because I am usually right. Anyway, in my capacity as Second Employee's Familiar Without Paperwork, I'm here to deal with difficult life situations such as this: so I am here PACING and SQUEAKING when Second Employee goes to bed, when someone rings her two hours later and she gets up again to drive to the hospital, and when she reappears looking stunned at five am saying, Ghostycat, you are very much A Presence. Yes I am. And I imagine I must be an enormous comfort, much more so than Esso with his Nuzzling!

So, I may be temporarily Suspending All Things, but I have made it Very Clear to Second Employee that this will not be for ever, and Strategic Plan Delivery must recommence ASAP!

## February 2025

Larry, sometimes Second Employee says to me, there is not one single unwonky lampshade in this house, Mr Esso *Puss Puss Cat*, and *I know why*. What can she possibly mean? It's an unsolvable mystery! Perhaps you could ask the Catinet. Esso

# Chapter 11
# Spring 2025: We have to be Terribly Supportive

**March 2025**

Larry, this is Ghost, Ambassador to the High Peak and Minister for Aesthetic Standards with a Very Serious Report. Well, Larry, as you know, I had to suspend Second Employee's KPIs while Second Employee's Father was very ill: unfortunately, he was so ill that now he has died, which is selfish because it means I have had to suspend them for even longer, until after the funeral. Which I thought might happen, but which is still Very Annoying, because KPIs do not deliver themselves.

Esso says, Ghost, if you begrudge extending the current emergency measures by another mere fortnight then I literally do not believe you have a heart *at all*. But, Larry, Esso is wrong (and also possibly feeling guilty about past teeth-related events which we are *apparently* all now supposed to forget): I do have a heart. It is just that someone has to keep things at the Embassy moving. Should I just let Second Employee wander round being sad and brooding? Of course I shouldn't. It is bad for her. And there is work to be done. Also, as Esso points out, organising a funeral 'takes some doing', and Second Employee will be busy until that is over: so, if I try to make her do two things at once, not only will we have no KPIs delivered at this difficult time, but we will also have whatever motley selection of people rock up at the wake presented with nothing but an unimaginative sandwich platter and a small pork pie instead of Competent Catering.

I do not think it makes me a Heartless Ambassador that I am focusing on the Practicalities. Wake-Goers must be Fed. And someone, for God's sake, must try to remember if Second Employee's Father had a favourite Hymn or any kind of Faith or Religion At All, so they can work out whether the service should talk about God, or just look shifty in the bits where one might expect it to do so: rather than focusing on Ridiculous Things like his Affection for his Family and Nice Cups of Tea, which are things which are not Cerebral. Besides, I have assured Second Employee that there is a place in the Afterwards for her Father, who was a kind soul: and she need not worry about that side of things.

[Note from Ghost: I did go slightly beyond my remit here, I suppose, technically. Esso said, Ghost, you cannot go promising plum places in the Afterwards willy-nilly when there is a process to go through and we need to fill in a form. But it has all been fine. Second Employee's Father really has not caused any trouble at all. In fact his Local History Society meetings have been very successful, due *in large part* to the quality of the tea and biscuits. It always surprises me how popular biscuits are in the Afterwards.]

So I really think I am being very supportive, and organising things well. And the other supportive thing I have done is, I have decided not to send Second Employee an email asking her what five things she has achieved this week, and sacking her if she cannot answer satisfactorily, even though I admire Elon Musk's approach to staff management ENORMOUSLY! And it is such a MASSIVE SHAME that I cannot (yet) put such a wonderful idea into practice! But I think we have to be Inefficient for a couple more weeks, Larry: although, after that, I am hoping we can get right back on with delivering the Strategic Plan!

[Note from Ghost: I will just add at this juncture that Second Employee's Family were not even able to get a person Transitioned Properly from This World To The Afterwards without Drama. First, Covid broke out in the hospital, and they all had to wear Plastic Gloves and Aprons and dispose of them properly in specified bins, which Second Employee found very confusing and which made her laugh inappropriately. Then Norovirus broke out, and Second Employee said it was very lucky that she had inherited her father's Severe OCD, because she washed her hands neurotically and managed not to get it:

Second Employee's Uncle and Brother, however, despite also washing diligently, came down with it one after the other; so I personally think that what saved Second Employee was Mere Luck.

Then everyone Took Against the Man In The Next Bed, who, I understand, was behaving like a Loud Middle Class Entitled Arse, Particularly With Regards To Weetabix: but First Employee said, perhaps he was behaving that way because he was frightened; because sometimes that is how middle class men of a certain age act when they are frightened. And then everyone looked at First Employee, who is *also* middle class, rather thoughtfully, and contemplated what he would be like at the Transition Time himself: and so Second Employee's Brother *formally banned anyone else from dying* until everyone had again worked up the energy to do all-night vigils, sitting in the Chesterfield Royal Hospital Costa Concession at Odd Times, Eating Sausage Rolls Despairingly in the main concourse, and Driving Down To The Ward at 100mph at three in the morning for emergencies. Well, as you know, Second Employee's Brother and I have had our differences mainly caused by me being right and him being wrong: but for once I think he has taken the correct action. I applaud it.]

**March 2025**

Larry and the Catinet: this is Esso, Ambassador to the High Peak. Larry, Second Employee's Father's Funeral is next week, so we will soon be welcoming House Guests. I have warned Ghost and both the Employees to take Particular Care of what their Teeth Are Doing, because I really feel at the moment that Biting Won't Help Things, and of course no-one need ever be the least concerned about mine!

**March 2025**

Larry, this is Ghost, Ambassador to the High Peak and Minister for Aesthetic Standards, with an update. Today I have been relaxing on a background of grey linen: occasionally, in some lights, I have noticed that this particular weave can look a little multicoloured, but obviously be assured, in case anyone ever says anything to the contrary, that it is not true. I would never lower myself to sit on anything Unaesthetic.

Well, Larry, no-one has covered themselves in glory recently, especially Second Employee and Esso. We have at least managed to get Second Employee's Father's Funeral successfully completed. Second Employee is pleased with herself because she says, and I quote, everyone enjoyed the Sausage Rolls and Scotch Eggs at the wake and also her eulogy 'which had funny bits in it'. I shall leave you, Larry, to wince alongside me at the picture of Failed Dignity and Lack Of Protocol this creates. At least, I suppose, Second Employee's Brother didn't feel inspired to whip out an easel and paint one of the sausage rolls for posterity (at least, as far as I know he didn't, although who can guarantee anything with that family!).

Esso says he personally is *enormously* grateful that Second Employee did the eulogy herself, as if it had been Second Employee's Mother she might well have Denounced Esso From The Cemetery Lectern As A Naughty Naughty Biter. Well this is true. I think she definitely would have done, frankly. But, Larry, Esso does not help himself. The night before the Funeral, a selection of Second Employee's Family came to stay, and Esso's beanbag was Temporarily Relocated so there was enough room for everyone to sit down. This had been approved in advance: we had all agreed it was the only way, given the Space Limitations in the Embassy: but, Larry, Esso did not cope well. He kept going out and coming back in again to look very firmly at Second Employee's Family to see if they had *entirely independently* decided that they wanted to move yet. However, there was nowhere for them to move to: so he then walked up and down on them all to see if they were still happy with their life choices and the decisions they were making. Esso is a large cat, and this made them nervous: so his next trick was to sit where his beanbag normally was anyway, and to look solid and intimidating, getting under everyone's feet. Second Employee snuck downstairs after everyone had gone to bed to put his beanbag back for him, and then he glued himself to it metaphorically and refused to move for the next forty eight hours, despite it meaning not enough seats, and so people having to stand up on a kind of rota. So I really feel, Larry, that Esso's actions made the situation worse and did nothing to ameliorate his reputation as the Bad Cat Who Had Bitten The Deceased. That is my opinion.

Of course, Esso sees it quite differently. He sees it as 'staying by her side to support Second Employee', and believes all these things are merely a matter of interpretation - but then he also thinks I looked earlier as if I was sitting on CROCHET, which as we all know is nonsense, because I explained that particular situation in my *very first paragraph!* Anyway, despite Second Employee having been Mildly Ridiculous by walking into an Aerial Hoop and nearly breaking her nose, which has put us back a further couple of days, I really think we are now FINALLY back on track to start again with delivery of the Strategic Plan!

**April 2025**

Larry, this is Ghost, Ambassador to the High Peak and Minister for Aesthetic Standards. Larry, can you just update the Register of Member Interests with the fact that Interim Summer Employee now lives next door, in the Flat which was my Meditation Space until the Employees allowed a Silly Man to live in it. Well, now we have got another Silly Man living in it, but, as Esso says, at least it is *our* Silly Man, because it is Interim Summer Employee.

Larry, Esso is very pleased; because Interim Summer Employee leaves his front door open when he is home so we can visit easily, which Esso says is very kind, although Lokie From Three Doors Down has taken it as permission for him to visit as well *which it is not;* so Esso sometimes has to Fluff His Tail Right Up to scare him off. And it *is* kind: but I am anxious that if I go in to sit on the nice grey carpet and look at the nice white walls Interim Summer Employee might pick me up *on purpose,* and tickle me and kiss me. Because he has form for doing this, frankly, and it has been witnessed. So what I am doing at the moment is staying on the side of the Embassy and, when Interim Summer Employee POPS UP to click his tongue and pspsps at me, I ROLL onto my back and I show him my Furry Underneath, which I imagine must be deeply intimidating for him: and in this way, my dignity is maintained. I am monitoring the situation daily, Larry, and if I find there is a way to enter safely and enjoy the nice white walls I will do so.

## April 2025

Larry, this is Ghost, Ambassador to the High Peak and Minister for Aesthetic Standards with an IMPORTANT WARNING to the Catinet. Larry, I have been saying to Esso ever since Second

Employee's Father Died that we should update the risk register to take into account the new status of Second Employee's Mother. Because now she is no longer a carer she is effectively on the LOOSE: and she will not be content roaming round Chesterfield Marks and Spencer for ever, especially given that it hasn't got a cafe since it moved to the retail park. No. She is clearly going to venture further afield.

Well, Larry, Esso said, there is no rush, Ghost, we will leave things to settle down for a bit and everything will be fine. HOWEVER! He was running very fast up and down the sitting room the other day waiting for his teeth to decide on their next steps when suddenly Second Employee's Mother walked right into the room, bold as brass and shameless as you please! Esso said when he saw her he screeched to a halt, right on the rug. He looked at Second Employee's Mother. She looked at him. He says he is *literally convinced* that he heard Graham next door start up playing some Ennio Morricone, which I PERSONALLY think is vanishingly unlikely given that Graham is a modern jazz violinist and doesn't own a harmonica, but Esso says he *knows what he knows*. He says they stared at each other, and Second Employee's Mother said to him, well then Mr Esso, I hope you're not thinking you're going to bite people. Because it didn't go so well for you with the last one, did it: given that he DIED!

Esso says that in *all his born days* he has never had an Employee's Mother stride into his room and accuse him of Deliberate Actual Murder before, and he will probably never get over it. He has been lying down to try to muster his resources but he says he cannot even begin to think about the Strategic Plan until he has at least had an apology.

Well, Larry, obviously this is terrible news for me, given that the likelihood of Second Employee's Mother apologising for anything is similar to the likelihood of Angela Rayner running off with Rupert Lowe and either of them enjoying it. So I have urgently visited the Goats, who are living in a really lovely stone cottage just on the edge of the Thornbridge estate, terribly Country Living meets Cottagecore with hand stencilling above all the dadoes and their vegetable garden really is fabulous; but I *do not want this*! I want WAR! Anyway Alejandro said to me, look, Ghost, WAR just isn't where we are right now, especially now I'm Treasurer for the Ashford In The Water Women's and Goats' Institute and everyone admires my courgette pickle so much; but I'd be really happy to facilitate some kind of Mediation involving Second Employee's Mother and Esso, perhaps ending in a therapeutic diamond painting session and a group hug. Larry, this is not what I want! I need firm action and Vengeance! Please deal with Esso, the Goats, and Second Employee's Mother for me, and I promise that by this time next week we will have made amazing progress on the Strategic Plan and even signed off the first quarter!

## April 2025

Larry, this is Ghost, Ambassador to the High Peak with an Emergency Bulletin. Larry, this is an Emerging Situation, but what we *do* know is that apparently Second Employee DID have a 'job' in Chesterfield, quite unbelievably: but that she does no longer: because she has 'told them to stick it right up their bum'. Esso says what if she is going through a Fighty Phase and also tells us to stick her job here up our collective bums, and I have said, Esso, we have all seen so much of your bum that we are quite fed up of it; so I hardly think Second Employee would want to spend her free time discussing it as well.

So that is my final word on that! And I have made it very clear to Second Employee that she must stop being FLAKY, knuckle down, and attend to her KPIs. So you and the Catinet can be quite assured that I, at least, am managing the situation appropriately!

## April 2025

Larry, this is Esso, Ambassador to the High Peak. Things are not going well today, Larry. The gearbox has gone on the Peugeot again and the Employees are grinding their teeth. Also a new Employee Bed has been delivered, which

Discombobulated Ghost and made her MEW at Second Employee and seek out the Crochet Blanket to KNEAD on for reassurance. First Employee has diagnosed himself via Chat GPT as having 'irritated his IT band' and will *not* stop telling us about it. And what's more, Second Employee says she has 'fallen head first into cake and doesn't care' even though she is 'staring right down the barrel of a gun' with regards to the Chesterfield 10K in thirteen days time, which her brother is not letting her drop out of despite the fact that her ex-boss will be there, and she is quite untrained apart from a failed 'fell run' seven days ago which involved getting lost in a forest and ending up in a farmer called Alan's front yard being GOOSED by 'a dog who was as big as a donkey'. So as you can see, Larry, things are very, very serious; but unfortunately I have been almost entirely taken over by the PURR tonight so we will have to deal with it all properly tomorrow!

[Note from Esso: it is my understanding that Second Employee and her Brother Completed the 10K, but that Second Employee was in a Particularly Fighty Mood, and at one point strode up to a woman who had kindly made a sign to encourage the runners which said 'you're amazing!' and said to her loudly, no, I bloody am not, I'm only doing this because my brother made me and actually I hate him. I understand further that she was at one point Heckled by a Man, who shouted, Well Done Duck but try and start running again when you get to those traffic lights, and instead of receiving this politely she shouted back loudly Oo

Aye, Mate, I will if you will. I was relieved, however, to learn that although she was practically standing next to her ex-boss at the start line, her brother managed to manoeuvre her out of the way so she was standing behind someone who was dressed as a Wolf, and so they did not see each other. I am very glad there was someone there to organise her.

We had a debrief, and if she does the 10K again next year she will not be rude to nice ladies with signs. She would like to make it clear that she saw a number of small children who also had signs, and in fact theirs had Sparkly Handprints on them and said, Hit Here For A Power Up!: and she Hit Here on Each One and said thank you very politely to each of the small children. I said to her, and did it power you up, and she said, no, because by that point only Strong Amphetamines or a Bear In Hot Pursuit could have made her go any faster. Indeed it would almost certainly have needed more than one bear, possibly working together. My conclusion from all this is that I am going to supervise very, very carefully any future Race Entries. In fact I have forbidden them UTTERLY for the moment.]

**May 2025**

Larry, this is Esso, Ambassador to the High Peak, Minister for the Maintenance in Impossible Circumstances of Aesthetic Standards, and Clever Deployer of Employees. Larry, there have been developments. Second Employee's Small Scruffy Blue Car is no more. It will not get through its next MOT. It has 'extensive corrosion on its undercarriage' (I have FORBIDDEN Ghost to make 'amusing' comparisons to Second Employee herself), and it is no longer cost-effective to repair.

We have to look at situations like this, Larry, with a calm and unemotional eye, which I have explained to Second Employee: but it hasn't worked, and she is Prostrate With Grief and 'cannot cope with any more loss this year'. It is the Last Straw. Apparently, Larry, Second Employee and the Small Scruffy Blue Car worked together on getting Second Employee out of the Bad Situation in Cambridge; and they travelled together on their joint bid for escape up the A14, listening to Revolver on the CD player, and got as far as Warboys before she became confused and had to park up in a pub and ring First Employee to come and rescue her and feed her Chocolate Digestives, Tunnocks Teacakes, and Strong Coffee.

And I personally think, Larry, that Second Employee's grief is not just about the Small Scruffy Blue Car and their adventures together, but is also about her father, and about all sorts of things that have changed and gone and happened over the last few years. So I further think, Larry, it will not respond well to Practicality at the moment; although Ghost is saying to me, for God's sake, Esso, too much thinking, just you tell Second

Employee to bloody pull herself together and at least *look* at the Gantt Chart and see what needs doing in the Next Quarter!

So, Larry, I have made an Important Decision. I have consulted with First Employee, and we have agreed that Second Employee is currently unemployable by anyone other than us: in fact, I actually think she is wandering about waiting for the opportunity to tell someone else to Stick Their Job Right Up Their Bum, so I feel a certain responsibility for protecting Buxton and the Local Area up to as far away as twenty five miles on the A6. To this end, I am *again* suspending Second Employee's KPIs. In fact, I have changed her Job Description *entirely* for the moment: I have made her the Embassy Archivist. I have TASKED her with collating and editing mine and Ghost's notes, updates and reports from the last few years.

I think it is time for us all to pause, look back and process before we go any further. There have been a lot of changes. For example, when Second Employee first decorated the Embassy, dark blue walls were fashionable: now they are not so much. Then, I didn't have a wonderful beanbag: now I do. Second Employee's Father was not in the Afterwards: now he is. All these things need to be thought about properly. And one or two things have happened politically as well, but they are nowhere near as important.

And of course, Larry, if I *were*, as a consequence of Second Employee's diligent ARCHIVING of my Bons Mots and Wise Words, to win the Pulitzer Prize for my Trenchant Commentary on the Most Important Aspects of the Cut and Thrust of Early Twenty Twenties Social Changes, I would try to meet that challenge with dignity. In fact, I may start working on my speech now. Just in case, you understand!

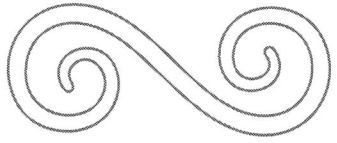

# About The Author

**Susie Halksworth**

Susie lives in Buxton with her husband and their Employers, Ghost and Esso. Ghost and Esso are *exactly* as they come across in this book.

Susie enjoys baking, crochet, dangling upside down on a hoop, and a number of other things which are not economically very productive.

She has a substack at susiehalksworth.substack.com where she posts new writing and other random bits, and would love you to follow her.

Printed in Dunstable, United Kingdom